Journe
Cr

The Career of DCI Sarah Rudd
from 2003 – 2008

by

Tony Drury

City Fiction

ISBN-13: 978-1-910040-12-6

THE SARAH RUDD CITY THRILLER SERIES

October, 2002

Detective Chief Inspector Sarah Rudd is one of the bravest police officers ever to patrol the streets of the Home Counties. Her later career is told initially in the books 'Megan's Game' and 'The Deal'. In 'Cholesterol' she is involved in a shooting in The Mall and saves the lives of the Royal Couple for which she is awarded the Queen's Police Medal for Gallantry. In 'A Flash of Lightning' she prevents the bombing of four hundred travellers in a London bound commuter train from a Jihadist attack. In 'The Lady Who Turned', published in 2014, DCI Sarah Rudd not only rescues her daughter Susie from a deranged kidnapper, but becomes a private investigator and fights off an East European gangster's attempt to take control of 'The Lady' magazine.

Sarah Rudd's early career is told in two books:

On Scene and Dealing - The Early Career of DCI Sarah Rudd

The title of the book is a message of arrival made by a police officer to Control when reaching an incident. Published in 2015, it is **Part One (**of two) telling Sarah Rudd's story from 1997, when she joins the Hertfordshire Constabulary as a probationary constable, to May 2003, when she becomes a detective. The ten separate stories each tell of various incidents in her early career as she matures into a respected police officer alongside her husband Nick, a schoolteacher, and Marcus, their son.

Journey to the Crown - The Career of DCI Sarah Rudd from 2003 - 2008

'The Crown' is a reference to the metal or embroidered insignia on a superintendent's epaulette. This is **Part Two** of Sarah Rudd's early career. It comprises eight stories charting her progress, initially from 2003 to 2005, when she passes her sergeant's examinations. In 2007 she becomes a sergeant and dedicates herself to gaining promotion to inspector and beyond in order to achieve the coveted crown. In 2008, the wheels fall off as she begins a destructive love affair.

JOURNEY TO THE CROWN
The Career of DCI Sarah Rudd from 2003 – 2008

Part One:

The Deskbound Detective - September 2003
The Case of the Missing Underwear - April 2004
The Killer Who Missed - June/July 2004
The Keys That Disappeared - April 2005
The Mysterious Case of 'The Mousetrap' - November 2005
A Matter of Time - February 2006
A Game of Two Halves - October 2006
In Spite of Overwhelming Obstacles - July 2007

Part Two:

An Accident in Timing - Summer 2008
The torrid relationship between Sergeant Sarah Rudd and Dr Martin Redding.

Part Three:

The Contract Killer - November 2015
A look ahead to the future of Sarah Rudd. She has left the police force, separated from her husband, and is now a private detective based in West London.

PART ONE

THE DESKBOUND DETECTIVE - SEPTEMBER 2003

Now safely back home, the legal executive sat shaking in her lounge. She slowly stood up and looked at herself in the mirror. The bruising and swelling were beginning to show. Her usually immaculate hair was a mess, her eye make-up was smudged, and mascara was running down her cheeks. She started crying. She wondered how it had come to this as she dialled '999'.

+

Detective Constable Sarah Rudd was thinking about the crown on Superintendent Dobson's epaulette.

She had been watching and coveting it as her superior officer held the door of the washroom open for her. Her pregnancy helped secure the courtesies of her colleagues. With five months already gone, she was displaying an impressive physique. The two colleagues had smiled at each other. Sarah reached her locker, changed her shoes and began the journey back to the Rudd house.

She reached home in time to pay the child-minder, who had already given Marcus his tea: muffins and jam. She looked at the cash remaining in her purse and tried to figure out where the fifty pounds she had drawn from the cash machine had gone. As she bathed her son she began to worry about the arrival home of her husband.

A little later, Sarah found herself staring at the pictures on the television. She picked up her glass of wine, put it down, and picked it up again. She walked over to her display of potted plants and poured it into the soil. She refocused on the Chancellor of the

1

Exchequer. The television was turned down because she could not stand his irritating and ingratiating tone of voice.

"If you're so bloody clever, mate, and you've eradicated boom and bust, how come the Rudd household has no money?" Their budgets were under increasing pressure from increases in their overheads: energy costs seemed to soar upwards. Her baby rumbled around in her womb and kicked her. She smiled as she anticipated the arrival of her daughter in about four months' time.

She picked up the pile of papers on the table. What had they done with the cash released by their Northern Rock Building Society re-mortgage? Why were the bills continually increasing: gas, electricity, water rates, insurances, food, clothing and the costs for Marcus, now three years and four months old? The row with Nick in the early hours of the morning still reverberated in her head. Their son was proving to be more expensive as they were unable to coordinate their work schedules to limit the cost of his care. Sarah had her unspoken doubts that Nick had the ambition to progress his career and justify the higher earnings of a head teacher.

+

The following morning, Sarah sat down in front of her boss.

Detective Inspector Eva Sutherland had arrived at Stevenage Police Station four weeks earlier. She had transferred from Plymouth after a four-year stay. The rumours circulating around the canteen suggested that she was talented, ambitious, and blazing an impressive career path: she had not yet achieved the higher rank to which she aspired but this move was a step nearer to the Metropolitan Police Force.

She was not, according to the internal news channels, married. She was somewhere between thirty and forty years old. She wore her dark brown hair cut short. She stared at DC Rudd and shook her head.

"You know the ropes, Sarah. You're on restricted duties until you start your maternity leave." She poured them both a cup of coffee.

Sarah raised her hand, "Water for me, please."

"Of course. Coffee's not a good idea. Right, off to the desk job," Sutherland smiled.

"But boss, I'll die of boredom just sitting there taking phone calls from retired colonels who think that their next door neighbour is a child molester."

"Just one call might lead to a result," suggested DI Sutherland. She smiled inwardly as Sarah stood up and slipped away from her office.

+

The call came through at eleven minutes past eleven o'clock. DC Rudd was told that a woman was insisting that she speak to a female officer. She was claiming that she had been attacked.

"How can I help you, madam?" asked Sarah as soon as the connection was made.

"I've been assaulted," replied the caller.

"What are your injuries?" asked Sarah, as she pondered the caller's surprisingly calm manner.

"I'll worry about them. I want you to arrest him."

Sarah drank some water. It was important that she maintained her fluid intake during the latter part of her pregnancy. Her daughter acknowledged the refreshments by kicking her.

"May I ask your name and address, please?" she continued.

"I've already given that to the other person. Mrs. Flora Williams, 26 Malvern Road. When will you arrest him?"

"Can I ask you again, Mrs. Williams, do you want me to call an ambulance for you?"

"I want you to arrest him!" she shouted.

Throughout her early years as a police officer, Sarah had developed a sixth sense. This, in part, reflected her growing experience and maturity but also an empathy with the public.

"I'm coming to see you, Mrs. Williams."

"When?"

"Now," she said as she put the receiver back on its holder.

Sarah recruited a Panda driver and they set off for Malvern Road on the south side of the town. Twenty minutes later, they parked the vehicle outside an imposing detached house in an affluent area of the community. The next-door property was for sale.

Sarah pressed the buzzer on the front door and then said, "Oh!" This was because she was looking at a dark haired woman who had appeared sporting a black eye.

"You need some help with that injury," said Sarah.

"Not now. Come in," ordered Mrs. Williams. Minutes later they were together in the lounge. The driver of the police car remained in the hallway. The rear window of the living area offered a view of the extensive back gardens with an immaculate lawn and several rockeries; there were two ornamental pools.

Sarah accepted the offer of a cup of tea.

"How long to go?" asked the victim of the alleged assault as she took in Sarah's physical appearance.

"Several more months," replied Sarah. She paused because she noticed that the woman was wincing and holding her left arm.

"Right. This stops here," she said.

She stood up and used her mobile phone to call for an ambulance. Mrs. Williams started to whimper.

"Can we call for help for you, Mrs. Williams? Your husband?"

"He left home some years ago."

"Your children?" Sarah had noticed the photographs around the room.

"My son is in New Zealand and my daughter is not speaking to me. She sided with her father."

"Neighbours?" asked Sarah.

"The house next door is empty. The owners' business went bankrupt. The other side are in East Africa."

"Friends?"

"When you've spent the whole of your working life building a legal business you don't have time for frivolities."

"What happened to you?" asked Sarah.

"I just want you to arrest him."

Sarah watched Mrs. Williams' quivering lips and felt that she needed to regain the initiative.

"You have been successful from what I see here," she continued.

"What a nice thing to say," exclaimed Mrs. Williams as she gasped with pain.

Sarah spotted the pulsating blue light and looked out of the window. She went to the front door where the driver had let in the medical team. The leader asked Mrs. Williams some questions, took her blood pressure, and carefully examined her arm. He then said that they were ready to leave. Sarah ascertained which hospital they would be going to and told Mrs. Williams that they would follow on behind. She would meet her again in the Accident and Emergency Department.

"One final question, please Mrs. Williams?" she asked.

"Just one," replied the injured lady.

"May I please look around your house?"

"Of course, my dear."

As the ambulance drove away, Sarah took the opportunity to begin to look over the property. It was immaculately kept with modern, if uninspiring, furnishings. Nothing was out of place.

In the kitchen she found a tea towel with some blood on it. She picked it up carefully and put it in an exhibit bag. In the dining room, she found some papers relating to a Coutts Bank deposit account. The credit balance showing made her whistle.

She looked at the bookshelves and found, among the titles, Bronte and Dickens, Martina Cole, Jackie Collins, and a 'History of Erotica'. She gave a cursory glance at the conservatory, which went out into the garden. She did, however, climb the stairs and spend a few minutes in the main bedroom and the ensuite. She observed the array of medicines and cosmetics. She studied Mrs. Williams' clothes and blinked at several of the outfits. Were they hers or did they belong to the departed daughter? Some of the underwear was rather adventurous for a lady probably in her sixties. She returned down to the hallway and

6

nodded at the police driver who opened the front door.

Sarah noticed that, although there was only one car parked at the side of the house, there were two sets of tyre tracks.

+

She reached the A & E department at the hospital and waited for nearly an hour before a doctor came to see her. They went into a side room and she closed the door.

"I'm Natalie McGiven. I'm the doctor on duty today," she said. "I'm told that you want to speak to me."

Sarah held out her warrant card. "DC Rudd," she said. "I went to Mrs. Williams' house this morning after she called in to us. Can you tell me how she is, please?"

Dr. McGiven wiped her eyes. She was reflecting a long night on duty with two stabbings amongst the usual traffic of emergency cases.

"She'll live," replied the doctor. "She'll be with us for several days because her kidneys have been bruised. Until she stops passing blood, she stays here."

"Is that the only serious damage?" asked Sarah.

"This is a strange case" mused the doctor. "Some of her injuries have been inflicted by another person. Obviously the black eye was caused most probably by a fist. The kidneys were possibly the result of several kicks. Her left arm is broken. There are some unusual injuries for a woman of her age." Dr. McGiven paused. "She's sixty-one. Her knuckles are bruised. I think she hit someone or something."

"What does that mean?" asked Sarah.

"As Mrs. Williams is refusing to answer any questions, I can only guess. She was complaining of pain down below and I think some fluid on her leg is probably dried semen."

"Is that it?" asked Sarah.

"The big toe on her left foot is broken. That will take time to heal," said Dr. McGiven.

"Can I see her?"

"We have sedated her. I'd prefer you come back later this afternoon." She looked down at Sarah's pregnancy. "How's junior?" she asked.

"I think I'm carrying Mike Tyson," laughed Sarah. "One final question, doctor, and thanks for your help. You say that Mrs. Williams has not said anything?"

"Oh, she's talking. She's demanding this and that. But she won't tell us anything personal, next of kin and so on, and she's remaining silent about how her injuries were caused."

"Time for some detective work," said Sarah.

"Can I suggest you ask a colleague," said Dr McGiven. "You look a bit tired. Hand her over, go home and get some rest."

"Not you as well," Sarah said to herself.

As they shook hands, the doctor smiled. "She has a tattoo. On the inside of her upper thigh. It's recent."

"A tattoo?" responded Sarah.

"It's a Chinese symbol. Most people will tell you it means 'love' but it means more than that. A Cantonese speaker would say it means 'lover' but even that is not quite right."

"What does it mean?"

"It means 'valentine'," said the doctor. "I was raised in Hong Kong. My father was a diplomat. I speak both Mandarin and Cantonese."

"As in Valentine's Day?" asked Sarah.

"In a way. Google it: it's all about the seventh day of the seventh month in the lunar calendar. Its position on her thigh suggests an intimate message."

"From whom?" Sarah asked out loud.

"You're the detective," said Dr. McGiven. "But please, go home and get some rest." She laughed. "That's doctor's orders."

+

Sarah finalised her notes, only to find DI Sutherland standing in front of her desk.

"I've been wondering where you were, Sarah. These desk jobs certainly move around." She picked up the notes and read them carefully. "Good summary," she said. "What is this all about?"

"I need to talk again to Mrs. Williams because there is probably an unsolved case of sexual assault. There is another person involved, presumably a man, and he might be dangerous."

"You're sure about this?"

"Some serious physical injuries and possible semen on her body, boss."

"Understood. But until Mrs. Williams presses charges, there is not too much we can do." She paused and smiled, "Go home Sarah. We'll take over from here." She stared at Sarah meaningfully, "Stay at home tomorrow."

+

Sarah looked at her watch. The day was passing

slowly. She realised that in less than an hour's time she would have to collect Marcus from the childminder. She therefore made her way to the staff canteen for a late lunch. She displayed strength of character in saying "no" to the fish and chips. She settled down to a green salad with grilled breast of chicken.

"May I please sit with the most adorable policewoman I have ever known?"

Sarah looked up and smiled. PC Jonny Willens could say what he wanted. A career copper with less than two years to serve until his pension kicked in. He had never wanted promotion. He was never offered promotion. But he was rock solid as a police officer, and he was popular. What he wanted to do was fish. He and his wife, a librarian, were planning their retirement holiday which would take in twenty-two rivers worldwide where Jonny would catch salmon and she would read Wilbur Smith books. They were starting with the River Dee in Scotland, then on to Iceland, to Russia and then East Asia. They would end up in South Africa where the author's greatest book 'When the Lion Feeds' is set. Mrs. Willens had read it at least five times.

"I may have to arrest you for harassment," laughed Sarah as they hugged each other. She always gave him the opportunity to talk about his fishing. She had even read one of Wilbur Smith's books because he talked about his wife's love of them so often.

They started talking as Jonny tucked into haddock and chips. Sarah groaned as she picked at her lettuce leaves. But Flora Williams was on her mind.

Jonny was a good listener. He put his hand over hers and patted it. "Come on, mate. Spit it out.

What's happening?"

Sarah went through the whole case with him. The hospital was keeping Mrs. Williams in and she continued to refuse to speak to the police officers who visited her. Jonny paid close attention to the details.

"DI Sutherland is right, Sarah. You're off the case."

She raised her eyebrows.

"Yes," said Jonny, "nobody tells DC Rudd anything!" He laughed. "Mrs. Williams is sixty-one years old, divorced, no kin that will come to her, a career woman. Move on, Sarah. It's somebody else's worry."

Sarah playfully slapped his face. "She's got lots of dosh, Jonny. Big, boring pad."

"What bra was she wearing?"

"Pardon?" exclaimed Sarah.

"You went round the house. I can't believe you did not take a women's interest in certain things."

"Well," laughed Sarah. "Since you ask. She uses push-ups." She chuckled seductively. "Some of us, Jonny, don't need them."

He failed in his attempt to appear contrite. "Look DC Rudd. I've already been cautioned for harassing you. This could get much more serious."

"The problem I have, Jonny, is that I'm too fat to run away from you."

They laughed together.

"Another question for you. In the bathroom. Lots of creams?"

"Jars of the stuff: an Aladdin's cave of cosmetics."

PC Willens paused and rubbed his chin with his hand. "I think she might be a cougar, Sarah."

"A what?"

"Any evidence of an American Express card?" he asked.

"There was an envelope on the table with their logo on it. How on earth did you know that, Jonny?"

"They all have them. She's a jilted career woman whose life has fallen apart. She's lonely and she needs sex so she's prowling the hotels and clubs looking for younger men. There are loads of websites but she almost certainly is a lone ranger."

"You're making this up," accused Sarah. "A cougar?"

"You know: Dustin Hoffman, 'The Graduate', 'Are you trying to seduce me, Mrs. Robinson?'"

Sarah opened her mouth in surprise. "Dreadful accent, Jonny," she said, "I think you should stick to the day job."

"Probably right. But I think I might be on to something." He finished his drink and stood up. "Duty calls. She's fallen out with somebody and they both got hurt." He thought carefully, "Did you pay her any compliments? Cougars love them."

Sarah shook her head in disbelief.

"How did you know that?" she thought to herself.

Jonny hugged her. "Take care, Sarah, and go home. Cougars survive; they're a tough breed. You've a baby to bring into this world."

He wandered off to think about the Rynder River in the Kola Peninsula situated in North Eastern Russia with its seventy-five named salmon pools. He shuddered as he thought of the Arctic temperatures ahead of him and his wife.

Sarah was also thoughtful. She was picturing herself back in the home of Flora Williams; the home of a cougar?

She remained at the table and pondered the facts. Jonny had made her think about the evidence: an older woman, financially well placed, a successful career, a letter from American Express, a bathroom full of wrinkle cream, push-up bras, serious injuries, and her reaction to the compliment that Sarah had paid her. Her baby turned over inside her.

A few more moments passed until her phone buzzed. She pressed the button and read the message.

"I think you might have caught a Sugar Mama. Take great care. Jonny."

Sarah returned to her office and researched the term. It meant a cougar, often a successful career woman, bitterly resentful about her divorce and the husband having a younger lover. The cougar, in certain circumstances, could become violent.

At that moment, Detective Constable Sarah Rudd realised the truth.

She closed her office door behind her and drove to the hospital. After a lot of arguing with the staff, she managed to have the patient moved into a side ward. Finally she was alone with Flora Williams.

"Thank you for coming. How's the baby?" asked the patient in a subdued voice.

"Where is he?" asked Sarah.

Mrs. Williams' eyes filled with tears. "I knew that you would guess," she whispered. "I just wanted to be held and loved. I'm alone in the world. It's not fair."

"I want his name and address, Flora," demanded Sarah.

"Rehan. Rehan Wilson. I met him in a Park Lane hotel. He was a wonderful lover." She reached for her box of tissues. "Then he started asking for money."

She started to shudder. "It got worse. Two weeks ago I think he slipped something into my drink because when I woke up I had this tattoo on my leg. He said he wanted me to know that he loved me." Her tears began to flow more freely. "He was insistent that he whip me but he's only a small man. We had a fight."

"Where is he, Flora?"

"Room 239. The Sudbury Hotel, off the A11. He's tied up. I also added a sleeping pill to his champagne. I put a 'do not disturb' notice on his door but they have probably found him by now." Flora Williams looked at Sarah. "What happens to me?" she asked.

Sarah stood up. "We'll want a statement, Mrs. Williams. That'll happen when your doctor says we can interview you. We'll also go and find Rehan Wilson. You will then be told what the next steps will be."

Flora Williams buried her head in the pillows and Sarah could see that she was still crying. She paused and looked at the distressed woman before leaving the room.

+

DI Sutherland raised her glass and smiled. "Well done, Sarah. Excellent armchair detective work," she commented.

They were in the wine bar adjacent to the Police Station. Rehan Wilson had been rescued from the hotel room and undergone treatment for a severely bruised testicle.

"Well, boss," said Sarah. "We DCs are only as good as our leaders. Thanks for having faith in me."

Sutherland beamed "What a pleasant thing to say,

Sarah. I really appreciate that."

Sarah thought that she was over-reacting. She had done her job. She realised that DI Sutherland was still talking.

"So, the doctor says you are fit and well."

"Yes. The blood pressure is up a little but I'm fine. Baby is good. Four more weeks and I'll call it a day."

"You'll come back, though?"

"Try and keep me away! There are probably some more cougars out there." They laughed together. "I also feel that I'm fortunate to be working with you, boss."

Eva Sutherland smiled and ran her hand through her hair. She pushed out her chest. She handed Sarah a credit card, "Show that and they'll put it on my bill."

Sara looked down at the piece of plastic in her hand.

"Go on, go and get us another drink, Sarah. I need some more champagne."

Sarah stood up and walked over to the bar. She looked again at the plastic in her hand.

It was an American Express Credit Card.

"You clever so-and-so, Jonny Willens," she said under her breath.

+ + +

THE CASE OF THE MISSING UNDERWEAR - APRIL 2004

The first note was posted through their letterbox in the middle of the night. The envelope was marked 'Private' and addressed to 'Nicholas Rudd'. The recipient was first down in the morning as the children had not disturbed his sleep. He opened it without thinking. He looked askance at the single sheet therein and the cut-out letters (taken from a magazine) which formed the message, 'Nicholas. You're so sexy.' There was a signature in italic handwriting, 'Love from Martha Greystoke.' He took it upstairs and showed it to his wife. "Kids!" he exclaimed.

+

Detective Constable Sarah Rudd rubbed her eyes. Where were her knickers? She paused and listened for any warning sounds coming from the kitchen. Susie, now eleven weeks old, was sleeping peacefully. Marcus, nearly four, was with the child minder. She could see the sheets, pillowcases, shirts, tea towels, socks, and male underpants all pegged to the washing line. What was missing were three pairs of knickers and two bras.

She wandered around the small back garden laid mainly to grass. There was little wind, and the spring warmth was beginning to banish memories of a cold winter. She had given birth to Susie without a problem and was back home in two days. Nick coped well with the ever-active Marcus. The grandparents did as much as they could.

The world of Sarah Rudd was complete. She had a hard-working schoolteacher husband, two children, reliable and supportive parents, and a job that she loved. Their finances were stretched but the Government was proclaiming strong economic conditions and so they'd rely on their credit cards and hope for something to happen in their favour.

She sensed that she was not alone. She looked around and there was the postman. Sandy was a proud Scotsman and a practical joker. He explained that he had a parcel for them and so he had come round to the back of the house. He handed over the box wrapped in brown paper and covered with official stamps.

"Marijuana from South America," he suggested.

"Don't be silly, Sandy, we've not finished the last lot you delivered," laughed Sarah. "Cup of tea?"

"No lassie, my shoes are wet. Cheerio."

She patted him on the shoulder and watched him limp away. She looked down at the package;

'Strictly confidential. Nicholas Rudd. Addressee only'.

She took it into the kitchen and found a magnifying glass. She tried to decipher the postmark. Perhaps 'Tromso'. She thought that was a town in Sweden but her Google search proved it was in Norway and famous for its northern lights, the 'aurora borealis'. She shook the package. She wondered whether it might contain CDs or perhaps DVDs. She placed it on the lounge mantelpiece.

She was missing three pairs of knickers and two bras. This produced another problem. She was now short of everyday underwear. She checked on Susie and moved the cover away from her mouth. She went upstairs and rummaged in her bedroom drawers. This produced six pairs of knickers and three bras. Problem solved: probably a local weirdo. She'd keep

18

an eye out for him.

The cause of the row between her and Nick that evening was what was so often on their agenda. The stresses of their financial pressures. The postman had delivered a letter from their building society reminding them that their period of interest-free payments would be ending in June. The new monthly repayments were nearly £600 higher. Nick had exploded and Sarah reminded him that he had taken out the new mortgage in the first place "to solve our fucking financial problems", she had shouted. He had exited the house, threatened the framework of the front door, and woken up both Marcus and Susie.

It was then that Sarah noticed that the package had been removed from the shelf. She checked the waste bin and there was no wrapping paper in there. She looked in the dustbin, which failed to reveal anything relevant.

Later that evening she and Nick slept back-to-back in a haze of alcohol odour. The next night resulted in further slamming of the doors and a retreat, by Nick, into the spare bedroom.

The second envelope came through the letterbox in the middle of the next night. Nick had got up for a drink of water at around 2.00pm and did not notice it. Susie started crying at 3.30pm and Sarah went downstairs to find the delivery on the floor. It had the same message on the envelope: 'Private: Nicholas Rudd'. She left it on the kitchen table. The next morning her husband opened it to find the same style of message in cut-out letters, 'Nicholas. You're a big boy'. The signature was the same, 'Love from Martha Greystoke'.

Two nights later another envelope was delivered in the same style with a similar message, 'Nicholas. You thrill me,' and the same signature in italic handwriting: 'Love from Martha Greystoke.'

That evening Sarah asked Nick about the three envelopes.

"School kid pranks," he replied.

Sarah frowned. "So you're happy that a demented schoolgirl is delivering these messages in the middle of the night?" she challenged.

"Nothing surprises me, Sarah," he replied and brushed off the rest of Sarah's attempted discussion of the matter.

Three days later, a bra and two pairs of knickers disappeared off the washing line in their back garden. Sarah was also coping with Marcus and his petulant reaction to Susie's arrival. Added to this, Nick seemed distracted. His son had developed a rash on his foot and Sarah thought it could be eczema. Nick had dismissed her judgement and said it was a heat rash. His wife pointed out that eczema was a rash.

Following the now standard exchange of caustic comments, he went down to the local surgery whereupon he was told by the doctor that it was a mild case of eczema. Marcus was given a prescription for a corticosteroid cream and a body lotion.

"I always thought that eczema was caused by stress," he said to the GP.

"It can be, Mr. Rudd. Marcus should be better quite quickly."

Nick stormed home and accused Sarah of creating tension in the house. They were to occupy separate rooms later that evening.

+

Sarah heard a familiar voice behind her.

"Did you find it?"

It was early the following morning and she discovered that Nick had already left for work; she arranged for a friend to take Marcus to playschool.

"Find what, Sandy?" Sarah asked her favourite postman.

"The parcel I left yesterday. You were out." He led her to the back garden and looked inside the shed. "Here it is, lassie," he shouted.

"You don't usually do this, Sandy," said Sarah.

"You dinna get many parcels," he answered.

She took the box inside and looked at the top of the address label.

'Strictly confidential. Nicholas Rudd. Addressee only.'

She used the magnifying glass to try to identify the postmark. The stamps had animals on them as well as foreign wording. She found 'Belgrade', the capital of Serbia. She again thought it contained CDs or DVDs. She put it on the hall table.

Susie started to cry, and so Sarah prepared a bottle of milk. Unfortunately she was unable to provide the feed herself. When Nick came home later that afternoon the parcel disappeared without trace.

That same night another letter was delivered to their house. Same addressee. Similar message:

'Nicholas, my hand is in a naughty place thinking about you. Love from Martha Greystoke.'

Three days later, a bra and two pairs of knickers were stolen from the washing line in the back garden of the Rudd household.

Detective Constable Sarah Rudd, despite being on

maternity leave, decided to solve the case herself. Her first thought was local kids. There was a path running behind the house at the bottom of the relatively small garden. It was used by local people as a link from the park to the main road. There was a gate that the Rudds used.

Sarah searched carefully but, with the ground dry after a relatively clement March, she could find no evidence of any unauthorised entry. There was a side passage to the garden from the front with an iron gate but the utility room window overlooked it. Sarah thought perhaps an intruder might sneak in once, but not three times. She put the washing out early as Susie usually woke her up at around 5.00am.

She reviewed the neighbours. Since the Eastmans moved, after the raucous party in June 2003 the newcomers had hardly communicated. There was an older couple and three daughters in their teens. Next door on the one side was a young couple, both solicitors, who left early and were quite private although always friendly. The other side hosted 'The Colonel' and his wife. Sarah was never sure that he had not taken part in the Charge of the Light Brigade and certainly she had no idea what he was talking about when he relived 'The War Years'. They were visited regularly by their grown-up children.

Sarah often tried to think laterally. So, who might be the most unlikely thief? She dismissed a silly idea – her husband, Nick? And what were these packages all about?

She went to answer a knock at the door.

"Need you to sign for this one, lassie," said Sandy.

Sarah again noticed his limp as he left the driveway. She looked at the parcel he had put into her hand. It was the same size, and again marked for Nick. The stamps were obscured by black postmarks, all of which were illegible.

But her thoughts were on her underwear. She took a reference book from the study bookshelf, looked up a certain topic that interested her, put Susie in her pram, and went shopping. She eventually found where to buy maple seeds. She returned home and completed the preparation by crushing them in a bowl. She selected one bra and one pair of knickers and covered them in her self-made itching power.

The next morning she hung them out and then had a row with Nick. A credit card statement had arrived in the post and he accused her of over-shopping. When calm was restored, she wheeled Susie into the back garden and saw that her bra and knickers had disappeared.

The weekend that followed was tense, with Nick sulking and Sarah immersed in looking after Susie and Marcus. Sarah and he managed two arguments: one over money and the second over their sleeping arrangements. Nick tried to lay claim to his conjugal rights only to be told by Sarah to join the modern world. He then suggested perhaps some show of affection, only to be abruptly rejected.

On Monday morning Sarah was outside wiping the windscreen of her car when Sandy the postman passed their driveway.

"Nothing for you today, lassie," he said before trying to hurry away.

Sarah's hand flew to her mouth. "Sandy," she exclaimed. "Why are you wearing gloves?"

He turned and faced her. "You put itching powder on them, didn't you?"

"You!" Sarah exclaimed.

She grabbed his arm and propelled him into the house although progress was slow. He yelled out as his leg was caught on the door. Finally Sarah had him in the kitchen where she poured him a scotch. She checked Susie and then sat down by the frightened man. She watched him down the drink.

"Sandy. Why?" she asked.

"You wanna know?" he said. He rolled up the right leg of his trousers. Sarah gasped. There was an inflamed scar running down from his knee to just above his ankle.

"Iraq War," he said. "Al-Faw peninsular. We were trying to secure the oil wells. One blew up and took me with it. I was invalided out and the doctors say my leg's healed. I canna afford to lose my job."

"My underwear, Sandy?"

"I canna sleep. I find that by holding the items to my face, it helps." He looked at Sarah. "Sorry, lassie, I was in the wrong."

There was a loud banging on the front door. Sarah rushed to answer it. The visitor was the Colonel from next door.

"Where's the bloody postman? I'm expecting my magazine. Drinking coffee with you: I spotted his bike outside. I'll have him cashiered."

He charged into the lounge where Sandy had remained with his leg exposed.

"Christ. What's that?" yelled the Colonel.

A few minutes later he had listened to the whole story. He wanted to know who was in charge of his regiment and what help Sandy had since received since being discharged. He then exploded again. "Your lucky day, sonny. I'm on the committee of the

SSAFA."

"The SSAFA, Colonel?" asked Sarah.

"Soldiers, Sailors, Airmen and Families Association," he replied.

"They didna help me, sir," said Sandy rolling down his trouser leg.

"You did not have the Colonel on your side, Private. Come on. You'll resign your job. You're not fit to work." He paused. "Private! Now!"

Sandy looked at Sarah who nodded and gave him a hug.

Three months later, Sandy was receiving an army pension and had a small flat in a home in Lincolnshire. He was already the Entertainments Officer. A tradition developed whereby on every Tuesday evening Sandy sang out his favourite song:

'We're Going to Hang Out the Washing on The Siegfried Line.'

A further letter was delivered in the early hours of the morning. Sarah had been up with Susie at 3.20am and it was not there then. Nick found it at 6.10am. He read the enclosure carefully:

'Nicholas. Here's a picture of my friend. She's abroad so don't bother to try to identify her. My body is like her shape but I'm a bit bigger. Would you like to have me, Nicholas?' It was signed 'Martha Greystoke' in the same classic script.

Even by their standards, the row that followed was volcanic.

"You are being stalked by a girl at your school, Nick. Get it sorted," ordered Sarah.

"Firstly, we don't know that. I teach over eighty-two different school children. It could be a lad playing the fool."

Sarah scowled. "It's a teenage girl with the hots for you. You must have some idea, Nick."

"You'll be accusing the art class next," he shouted.

"What art class?" asked Sarah.

"Marjorie is away this week. I'm sitting in for her. This is my second week. They just sit there painting pictures. No infatuated pupil there, Detective Constable Rudd," he shouted. He slammed the door and went to work.

That night another letter arrived.

'Nicholas. You're a big boy just as I like it. Signed, Martha Greystoke.'

PC Jonny Willens sipped his cup of coffee and grabbed at the chocolate cake.

"I don't think we're going to talk about salmon fishing or cougars today," he said.

"Thanks for calling in, Jonny. I need to talk to someone I can trust."

A few minutes later she had told him the whole story and shown her colleague the five letters that Nick had received.

"Jonny. Schoolteachers can have their careers wrecked by these girls. There's obviously one with a crush on Nick. He's not talking it seriously."

Jonny read each of the letters. "This is a matter for the school, Sarah," he said, "it must be a girl who Nick teaches." He paused. "I'm not a detective, anyway. Just a plain honest copper, that's me."

But at that point he stopped.

"Hang on," he said. "Sarah, please get some paper and a pen. Not a biro, a pen."

Sarah reappeared with the requested items and was

asked to sit down at the table.

"Take a piece of paper and sign your name."

"Full signature, Jonny?" she asked.

"Usual, as if you were signing a cheque."

Sarah did so.

"Turn it over and sign a second sheet," ordered her colleague.

Sarah did so and then a third time."

"Right. Look carefully at the three signatures. What do you see?" he asked.

Sarah studied the individual pieces of paper. "Three of my signatures," she said.

"Notice anything special?"

Sarah looked again. "Nope, more coffee?"

"Look again. Are they exactly the same?"

"They're mine, Jonny. You saw me do it," exclaimed Sarah. "Hang on. They're not the same." She held up one of her efforts. "Look at this, the curve on 'S' is more exaggerated. Isn't that strange?"

"It's a fact. Nobody ever signs exactly the same. There are always slight differences. Look at the signatures on the five letters to Nick. They are all exactly the same."

"What does this mean?" asked Sarah.

"It means, DC Rudd, that they've been signed by five different people who have meticulously copied the original." He paused. "This is not about one star-struck young lady. This is a group of kids having fun at Nick's expense; they're artistic as well, to be able to copy so accurately."

Sarah grabbed her phone and sent a text to her husband. *'It's the art class, Nick.'*

As PC Jonny Willens prepared to leave, Sarah hugged him.

"Glad to have been of service, ma'am." He chuckled as he left to think about his coming retirement.

+

The telephone call came at 6.20pm. It was Sarah's father. He announced that he and her mother were coming round.

"You should have said "no"," shouted Nick.

"It must be serious" said Sarah as she stood up and approached her husband. "Please, Nick. Things are bad enough. I can't face any more. It's going to be a lump, or hospital tests, or Dad's prostate or something they can't manage."

Nick put his hand to her face but said nothing.

Half an hour later the tray of tea was placed on the lounge table and the strawberry cake remained untouched.

"You think your Mother and I are fuddy-duddies, don't you Sarah?"

"Daddy, I love both of you. Nick does, Marcus does and Susie will."

"You think we don't know, don't you?"

Sarah's mother said nothing and played with her empty plate.

"You're in debt up to the ceiling, aren't you?"

Nick stood up. "Are you saying I'm not looking after your daughter properly?" he yelled.

"We took Marcus to the supermarket last Saturday. Every time we offered him something from the shelves he told us he was not allowed to have it."

Sarah went to the cupboard and took out a bottle of gin. She found three glasses and some tonic water and poured them each a drink. She handed her mother a glass of orange.

"I'll stick to the tea, darling," she said.

Her father coughed and took out an envelope. "Your mother and I went through bad times. The war years wrecked this country. I'm not sure who won." He sipped his drink. "When you two were married we took out a life policy in your favour, Sarah. In the event of either of our deaths you would inherit £25,000." He drank some more gin and tonic: Nick realised that he was becoming a little emotional.

"The problem for you is that both your mother and I are still alive and we're not planning on leaving, just yet."

"Daddy, that's exactly the way I want it! The money is not important," said Sarah.

"We realised this might happen. So we made it a 'with profits' life policy. Double the premium but it means it acquired a value. It matured last week." He stood up and went over to Sarah. He kissed her and handed her an envelope. She moved away and slowly opened it. She took out a cheque with the name of the insurance company across the top. She read the details:

Pay Sarah Florence Rudd £26,238.42p.

And then she collapsed into the arms of her father as she sobbed her heart out. Her mother joined in. Half an hour later they had each put their head around the bedroom door and watched Marcus sleeping peacefully. Sarah brought Susie down and they kissed and cuddled her.

Sarah's father shook Nick's hand and whispered in his ear, "She's just like her mother. Agree with all she says."

+

As they prepared for bed, Sarah realised that Nick had brought in the television set.

"You're not watching football, please, Nick."

"It *was* the art class, Sarah. Five girls having fun at my expense. The Head's sorting it out."

"So, I solved it?" asked Sarah, scrabbling for a compliment.

"Yes, in part. One of them called me 'Nicholas' today; I realised straight away that she was involved, so perhaps it was a joint cop?"

"So, how were they delivering the letters?" she asked. "We would have seen them."

"One of the girls has a boyfriend who was happy to oblige," he laughed.

She realised that he had taken out a brown package from his private drawer.

"Several colleagues have tried this. It's the aurora borealis lights set to music. It's supposed to be a fantastic turn-on. It's taken me three attempts to get the right version."

Sarah realised that Nick was settling down in their bed. She slipped next door.

"Aurora bloody borealis," she said to herself."

She prepared and went back into the bedroom having dimmed the lights. She was wearing red and black suspenders and stockings. She allowed her lace slip to fall to the ground. Nick nearly shot out of bed. He uttered an anticipatory moan of expectation.

And then Susie began to cry.

+ + +

30

THE KILLER WHO MISSED - JUNE/JULY 2004

Flashback: February 2003

PC Jonathan Robinson never took a backward step. He trod carefully on the icy pavement. As the door of the terraced property opened, he was forced to withstand a tidal wave of noxious odours. He could smell faeces, urine, putrid rubbish, and stale sweat amongst the compilation of human dross.

The word he had received was that the dog would be put out on the street at around 11.00am, just before the occupier was taken away and re-housed by the local authority. He pushed his way inside and gasped. The animal had literally eaten the room. The man was covered in sacking and shuffled to the rear door, which he opened. The black German Shepherd came for the police officer. He tore into him, biting his left calf muscle and the inside of his right thigh.

"He's called fuckin' Heroin," slurred the owner.

PC Robinson now had his hand on the dog's fur and was stroking it.

"Good boy, Ben," he said, quietly.

As he left with his dog he turned back, "He'll be called 'Ben' from now on," he said.

"Don't give a shit," sneered the dishevelled pensioner. He was scratching an infected rash on his face.

PC Robinson and trainee police dog, Ben, left the house. Jonathan opened the rear door of the police van and guided the German Shepherd into what would become his mobile home.

They were beginning a journey together which would end when their unique bond would be torn apart in the most horrific circumstances.

+

31

Flashback: May 2003

"Well, I don't get that," said Detective Constable Sarah Rudd as she sipped her mid-morning coffee. She stared at the police officer sitting opposite to her and sensed that her heart was pounding.

An intriguing relationship between a man and a woman is one based on crazed infatuation but which is restricted by an unspoken rulebook with lines never to be crossed. Sarah already fancied PC Jonathan Robinson despite the fact they had met on only a few occasions. She had seen him at several incidents. What added to his appeal was his self-confidence and an aura which she had noticed seemed to attach to the police dog handlers.

In the spring of 2003, the daylight hours were lengthening and the demands on the Hertfordshire police force ever increasing. The two police officers were in the busy canteen at Stevenage Police Station. There were a limited number of available places and Jonathan had readily agreed to Sarah's request that she join him. They were soon chatting away. PC Robinson was not interested in husbands and babies and the cost of childcare and whether the red spots were indicating a dose of chicken pox for her son.

"My first dog was a Belgian Malinois," he explained.

"A what?" spluttered Sarah as she tried to avoid spreading a cream doughnut over her face.

"How do you manage it, Sarah?" asked Jonathan. "You've had a child, you eat like a horse and yet you've a perfect figure."

Sarah felt herself melting and quickly stuffed some more pastry into her mouth. She looked closely at her companion. She knew that dog handlers were often motivated and driven individuals; perhaps, by instinct, loners. Theirs was a 'dead man's shoes' world: waiting for a vacancy in the exclusive section. Then there would be a lengthy training period including an attachment to an experienced handler. They would learn 'tracking' wherein the animal was taught to expect a reward of food, or a toy, or being allowed to bite the target officer during training sessions. The dog was taught to respond to the spoken instruction, "pass auf": literally the German word for "look out" but to Ben it would translate as "chase and detain". This unique interpretation belonged to the police dog world.

Sarah was enjoying their time together.

"I don't really understand what you were saying about how you rescued your dog," she continued.

Jonathan laughed and wiped some cream off her face. "Keep eating and I will tell all," he said. "My first dog was called Abe. He was a Belgian Malinois: light brown in colour. They have short hair. They are wonderful for detection and defence. The US Secret Service uses them to guard the President in the White House."

"So what happened to Abe?"

"He died, far too early."

"On duty?"

"Diabetes." He hesitated, "I remember the vet telling me. He pronounced the words with some care. 'Your animal has diabetes mellitus' he said to me." PC Robinson wiped his forehead. "I should have realised sooner. He was peeing a lot and losing weight." He sighed, "But worst of all, I knew that he was depressed."

"You can tell if a dog is depressed?" asked Sarah.

"Of course you can," he responded.

"Oh. So they gave you another one?" said Sarah.

The canteen at Stevenage Police Station was almost full as the early shift was refuelling and preparing for the shoplifters, drunks, road rage incidents, and domestic disturbances which would occupy their May workday. There was a rapid turnover of police officers: tea-breaks were a brief period of relaxation in their crowded day.

"We have to find our own," said Jonathan.

Sarah stopped eating and stared again at her companion. Police dog handlers were an elite section of the police force. They were motivated and driven and respected by their peers. Police officers knew the effect of the dog handler and his animal arriving at a violent scene. The cessation of aggression from the thugs was remarkable.

"To save costs, I suppose?" she suggested.

"Nothing to do with it, Sarah." Jonathan sipped his coffee. "Hertfordshire Police does not have their own breeding programme." He paused again. "I also think our way is better. The choice of animal is so important. I'd not want one forced on me."

"Why?" asked Sarah.

"Do you know what is meant by 'goes down the lead'?"

"No. What does that mean?" she asked.

"It's about the ultimate relationship between handler and dog. The animal develops the ability to sense the transmission of the officer's feelings. The link is the dog lead which joins them together."

"I'm thinking of putting my husband on a lead," laughed Sarah as she tried to cover up the fact she did not really understand what he was talking about.

"My sympathy is with him," said Jonathan, "Must be a nightmare being married to you."

She put her hand on his. "It is, mate. Just don't tell him; he still fancies me."

"Join the queue," said PC Robinson under his breath.

"'Goes down the lead' … what does that really mean?" she asked.

He was warming to his favourite subject. "The secret of dog handling is the relationship between the officer and the animal," he said. "It works best when the dog has developed the ability to sense a command. 'Goes down the lead' is a term dog handlers *use. It's the bond, if you like, that unites us." He paused. "I sometimes found that Abe was almost ahead of me in sensing a situation." He hesitated, "Most police dogs are male, for that reason."*

"What reason?" asked Sarah.

"Females are unpredictable."

She stared at her friend. "I hope we're talking about female dogs," she simmered.

"It's well understood," continued Jonathan, "bitches are moody. As a handler I must have complete confidence in my animal."

"It's a bloody dog, Jonathan," said Sarah.

"We work together. It's the only way to get results. They have six, perhaps seven, years' useful working life. The relationship is vital. We are licensed as a team. We are inspected once a month. If the trainer detects any weakness in either me or the dog, we'll lose our licence."

Sarah stood up and fetched some more refreshments; she glanced around to ensure a senior officer was not noticing her extended refreshment break. Jonathan was due to meet his girlfriend. PC Emily Preston was attracting considerable attention from the male predators but was getting frustrated at her inability to interest PC Robinson with any degree of attachment. She was due to experience another period of waiting.

Sarah replaced the coffee cups and opened the packet of bourbons she had purchased. Jonathan could not resist those.

"So, this dog you collected?" she asked.

"Abe died five months ago." He hesitated. "They usually recover from diabetes but not Abe." He swallowed before continuing. "I had a call one evening from a pal in Radlett. He knew I was looking and he told me a German Shepherd was being put out."

"What does that mean?" asked Sarah.

35

"A tenant was being re-housed and he let slip that his dog would be released the next morning. I went over and took the dog away. He's a challenge. He's been badly treated and beaten at times. But we've already started training together."

"What's his name?" she asked. "I presume he's a male dog as we females are so unreliable."

"Ben," he said.

"Ben," she repeated. "So where did you get 'Ben' from?"

"It was my Dad's middle name."

"How about 'Benjamin'?" suggested Sarah. "I'm sure that would have pleased your dad more."

Her attempted humour fell short of its mark. Jonathan noticed she was looking at her watch; break times were usually short and they had been together for some time.

"Too many syllables," he explained. "You usually only have a short time to give instructions. I must get to the dog in a single word. 'Ben' is ideal."

His audience still seemed perplexed.

"It's all about a sound," continued Jonathan. "The moment the animal hears 'Ben', and recognises the command, it will instantly be alert."

Sarah thought about this. "So, 'Sarah' is out?"

"Two syllables, female, moody, and unpredictable."

"You're a whizz with the charm, aren't you Police Constable Robinson?" she laughed.

"Sarah, if I told you what I'm really thinking, I'm likely to be suspended."

"Mmmm," she muttered, again looking at her watch. "Must go. Duty calls. See you, mate." She stood up and began to leave but then stopped and turned back. "Jonathan. How do you know that I'm moody and unpredictable?" she asked.

"Goes down the lead, Sarah," he said, smiling.

As she walked away and pushed past several of her colleagues, she looked back and saw that PC Robinson was *deep in thought. She was not to know that in a little more than a year's time she was to share his thoughts in a way she could never have anticipated.*

+

The Present Time

In June 2004, police resources were yet again under threat. A London-based firm of chartered accountants had been paid over six hundred thousand pounds to tell the chief constable absolutely nothing he did not already know. The population was increasing; multiracial groups, with a different set of rules, were expanding; and the public's expectations were exploding, driven on by a headline-crazy, anti-police media.

Early in the month, the former United States president, Ronald Reagan, died at the age of ninety-three. Not many people in Stevenage cared and even fewer remembered his films.

One who did was Harold Watson who lived with his sister on the west side of town. He sometimes travelled to London to seek out the old movies. His favourite was 'Prisoner of War', made in 1954, in which Reagan played an American officer, Webb Sloane, who volunteers to be captured by the North Koreans so he can investigate claims of abuse in POW camps.

Harold walked the streets of Soho and loved the darkness and solitude provided by its cinemas. On one occasion he managed to masturbate three times during two showings of 'Dirty Dancing' as he fantasised about the nubile body of sexy dancer

Jennifer Grey.

Watson was known to the medical authorities, the police, and social services. He didn't work and was believed to be supported by his sister, Mrs. Moira Rains, whose husband had long gone. He was considered by some to be nasty and unpleasant and yet he maintained a clean record. There were no accusations of child abuse, and the regulars at the two public houses in which he drank all thought he was simply lonely. He went on holiday three times a year and the labels on his suitcase revealed the same destination on each occasion. What he did in Bangkok was not known.

Police Intelligence had marked down Harold Watson as a possible 'suicide by cop' individual. This was the label given to a person who wanted to die by being shot by the police. He had made several attempts to kill himself and on one occasion had stood on top of a town centre building for nearly three hours before being negotiated down. He was referred for psychotherapy but nothing seemed to change him. The categorisation given to him by the police followed an incident involving DC Rudd.

She was called to a possible disturbance when his sister panicked and dialled 999. DC Rudd spent about an hour in the house and talked at some length to Watson himself. She became convinced that he was thinking about engineering a situation where the police shot him. The house had been searched and no firearm discovered. She submitted all the intelligence she had gained before she went off duty.

In the early evening of Thursday 24 June 2004, Oscar One, the Force control room inspector, received a call involving firearms. As the Gold

Commander, he dispatched two armed response vehicles to the west of Stevenage. The police tactical approach was 'containment'. The report came from Mrs. Moira Rains, who had fled her house, saying that her brother had a shotgun. Inspector Meredith asked for the police intelligence system to be interrogated about Harold Watson. He noted the link with DC Sarah Rudd and put out a call for her. It was reported that she was taking a break in the canteen. He instructed that she should go immediately to the incident.

When the first ARV arrived at the cul-de-sac where the house was situated, Harold Watson opened an upper window and fired a shot. As the incident was reported, Oscar One – Inspector Meredith – immediately passed Gold Command to Superintendent Kinson. He became Silver and the lead investigation officer at the crime scene was Bronze. That was the police command structure: Gold, Silver and Bronze. Gold decides on strategy and, before long, he was being advised by a firearms trainer on possible tactics to be followed.

The lead officer, PC Andrew Smith (Bronze), had ordered his officers to the front and back of the house. Elsewhere the area was being evacuated and cordoned off. DC Sarah Rudd had now arrived and was talking to Mrs. Rains in a secure area. The negotiator arrived at 7.20pm.

PC Jonathan Robinson reached the incident and deployed with police dog Ben. He situated them near to the Bronze firearms officer who was behind the ARV at the front of the house.

"Here we go again," thought Jonathan.

He suspected that what lay ahead was a number of

hours during which officers would try to appease an attention seeker. If the police intelligence was wrong and he was not in the 'suicide by cop' category, the incident would end with the police being forced to agree not to prosecute and left ensuring Harold Watson soaked the medical and social services for all he was worth.

Jonathan knew he had to keep his cynicism to himself.

He looked down at Ben. He could hardly believe that the half-starved, flea-bitten wretch he had found at the house sixteen months ago had matured into a beautifully muscled beast with a black shimmering coat. Ben leant into him, and Jonathan savoured their friendship. It was the result of hours together forging a deep bond. He rubbed behind his ear.

"Good boy, Ben," he whispered.

+

Sarah Rudd spotted Jonathan and allowed her heart to sink just a little. She was returning after a final debrief with Mrs. Rains who had been taken away from the scene. She was not willing to try to talk to her brother and Sarah recommended they did not go that route. The local doctor had arrived and said that he had been treating Watson for depression. Overall there was no evidence of any abnormal behaviour and nobody could work out from where he had acquired a shotgun. The negotiator was trying hard to establish contact but Harold Watson had drawn all the curtains in the house and was not responding.

It was Sarah who offered some intelligence to the Gold Commander: she predicted that Watson would come out and hope to be shot. She withstood some fierce questioning by using a completely logical approach.

"We know he's suicidal. He's depressed. He's got a shotgun. He wants to die. We should wait."

"For what?" asked an officer.

"He'll come out," said Sarah.

As darkness fell, sighs of relief greeted the sighting of 'Teapot 1', the name given to the refreshment van, which had arrived to support the heavy police presence. Sarah found herself sitting behind a wall when a familiar voice asked to join her.

"Jonathan," she smiled. "Where's Benjamin, having his supper?"

PC Robinson laughed. "He's resting. He's never fed when on duty, Sarah. Dogs, and particularly German Shepherds, are susceptible to the risk of stomach torsions if they exercise too soon after eating."

He paused and then stood up. "We'll be going back shortly, as you seem to be influencing police tactics."

"Watson will come out, Jonathan," she said. "We women may be unpredictable but just trust our intuition." She paused. "Why do we need a police dog?" she asked.

"Forty-two good reasons," he replied.

"I'd have thought one was sufficient," she joked.

"Ben has forty-two teeth. If Watson tries to run, he'll bring him down quicker than any of us."

"Does he clean them every day?" said Sarah. She looked at her friend and noted his look of bemusement. She hurried to explain her feelings. "To be honest with you, Jonathan, it's the only way I can

41

deal with these situations: resorting to humour. Mrs. Rains is in pieces, Watson wants to die, and I'm going to have another argument with my husband over my late hours."

"Do you have to stay?" he asked.

"I've promised Mrs. Rains I'll do all I can to save her brother. I'm here to the end." She put her coffee cup down on the grass. "So, tell me about Ben."

"Abe was good but Ben is amazing. He's unbelievably intelligent."

"How is your girlfriend?" asked Sarah, who decided to change the subject. "I heard something about PC Emily Preston looking radiant."

Jonathan laughed. "She's got the looks and we're close but she's pushing me." He sighed. "Last night she said I smelt of Ben."

"Have you thought of taking off your uniform before you get into bed with her?" asked Sarah. "No, don't tell me," she continued, "you've been trying a threesome: you, Emily, and Ben."

"It is an occupational hazard," he said. "We never really manage to lose the smell of our animals."

Sarah laughed, "Perhaps the chief constable should issue an edict saying there will be female dog handlers in future. Then you can marry each other: the odour will be a unique aphrodisiac."

Jonathan looked at her and shook his head.

Sarah stood up. "Back to work," she said.

+

The whole area lapsed into silence. Nothing was happening. The negotiator was unable to secure any contact with the armed man inside the house. The curtains remained drawn and there was no visible movement. The police officers remained alert, knowing something might occur, but nothing did happen.

PC Robinson and Ben remained behind the front line. Sarah had also settled down to watch, not far away. It was mild and dry and quiet.

Time dragged on. They waited and waited. Cups of tea were handed around and packs of sandwiches were distributed. Sarah was thinking about her husband; she missed his warmth and companionship – despite the rows, she tried to remain as committed to his happiness as ever.

Jonathan had his hand on the back of Ben's neck and was playing with his fur. He knew that his animal never tired of attention. He sensed that Ben was stirring.

Suddenly, the front door of the house flew open and Harold Watson came out holding a shotgun at his side. The air was immediately full of a cacophony of sound as both firearms officers challenged the man to drop his weapon. The Bronze firearms officer shouted that he was going to Level 2 and Jonathan knew that this meant he was deploying the baton gun that would discharge rubber bullets.

The charge exploded close to Jonathan's head as the baton round exited the weapon. He watched as everything appeared to go into slow motion. As the gun was fired, the potential suicide twisted his upper body slightly causing the missile to glance off his ribcage and fly up into the air.

Watson was now facing Bronze and the police dog handler: Jonathan saw the barrel of the shotgun being raised towards their position. He sensed that the firearms officer was struggling to swap the baton gun for his Heckler & Koch MP5 9mm submachine weapon in order to deal with what was now a lethal threat.

"DOG," shouted the firearms officer, indicating an urgent need to deploy the German Shepherd. "DOG, DOG."

Jonathan could feel Ben's aggression and power down the lead: he shouted the attack command "pass auf" and released the dog. Ben flew towards Watson as Jonathan was transfixed by the rising gun barrel. As it levelled he sensed something devastating and inevitable was about to happen.

There was then the sound of both barrels of the gun discharging. He realised that he was uninjured. He saw that Watson was down in the street, lying on his back with Ben on top of him. The dog's teeth were around the top of the arm that had been holding the weapon. Harold Watson began to scream.

The Bronze firearms officer shouted out instructions. "Moving forward," he commanded.

Jonathan fell in behind him. The whole police presence seemed to inch ahead as though choreographed.

Watson was still screaming. The first officer cleared the shotgun away from his right arm which was still being held by Ben. The officer red-dotted him with a Taser which he would use if Watson resisted. Jonathan ordered Ben to release his grip.

It was then that he saw the ever-increasing pool of crimson blood spreading out from under the dog. He took hold of his collar and gently pulled him backwards. Ben tried to follow instructions but was losing his balance. As he fell on his side, a horrendous injury to his underbelly became visible.

Jonathan picked him up in his arms and withdrew. He sat down on the kerbside as the tears poured down his face. The other officers left him alone.

Sarah watched and worked hard to hide her own emotions.

Jonathan whispered into his dog's ear. "Good boy, Ben. Good boy."

They were the last words that police dog Ben was to hear.

Watson was led away, shaken and laughing.

+

Aftermath

Jonathan Robinson, despite an overpowering wish to retain his innate professionalism, was finding himself torn apart by recent events. His sleeping pattern was being assailed by the memories of the death of Abe. He could, and should, have detected the destruction caused by diabetes. He shuddered and threw the bedclothes off as he reflected on the weight loss that he failed to investigate.

The end of Ben was different. He died in the line of duty. It was his job to go in and subdue Harold Watson. It is probable that he saved other officers from injury or even death. The firearms officer had experienced problems in releasing his MP5. There were other armed police but it was the speed with which Ben reached Watson which mattered in the end.

Jonathan could not forget the shredded stomach of his partner.

He had visited his mother in the care home but she was unable to understand what he was trying to discuss with her. There were the matters of an outstanding prescription that needed collecting, her hearing aid which required a new battery, and that she had an in-growing toenail.

He smoothed the sheets of the bed, kissed her gently, and left the building; he felt rather alone. He went back home to face another night of recriminations.

+

The ladies' cloakroom at Stevenage Police Station was a hub of rumour, misinformation, and gossip. It was not unknown for a woman to hear that she was having an affair with an Inspector who she had never met.

Sarah was too preoccupied with her career ambitions and demanding family life to become involved. On this occasion, however, she could hardly avoid the high-pitched squealing of two of her younger colleagues. She prolonged the drying of her hands because of a name that she was hearing.

PC Emily Preston was standing a few yards away and facing a blond colleague. "Crap. He didn't stand me up. Jonathan's missing his dog," she hissed.

Her companion laughed in her face. "Poor little Emily. Ditched for a hound," she sneered.

"For fuck's sake, Zoe, the thing was shot to pieces," Emily retorted.

"The truth is that he doesn't fancy you," said Zoe.

Sarah decided to leave them to their altercation banter but hesitated as she heard Emily Preston's response.

"I suspect he might chuck it all in."

+

Postscript

Six days later, Sarah asked Jonathan to join her for a stroll in the local park. She was pleased by the immediate text of acceptance which he sent to her.

"Did we do anything wrong?" she asked as they walked together.

Jonathan looked straight ahead. "No. It was a textbook operation. Watson was attention seeking." He paused, and Sarah wondered if he was wiping an eye. "Ben was almost too quick for him," he continued. "I think he fired the shotgun in surprise as much as anything."

"Where's his grave?" she asked.

"He was taken to the vet who will have disposed of the body."

Sarah walked in silence for about forty yards. The area was rather noisy with school children playing games and begging for ice creams. "So, time for the next dog," she suggested.

"Let's sit down," replied Jonathan.

They found an unoccupied bench seat in a quiet area away from the kids.

"I'm struggling, Sarah, but you know that, don't you?"

Sarah looked closely at her friend. "You're a highly-trained dog handler, Jonathan. It goes with the territory. Snap out of this and find yourself another dog."

He turned and faced her. His eyes were sad and there were tired lines on his forehead. "I've lost two now, Sarah. I know you once said, 'it's a bloody dog', and you're right." He held her hand. "But just think of what being a police dog handler means: the years of training together, the dangers and spills, and the monthly reviews. I know that we're respected by other officers but it's one hell of a lonely role."

"And rejected by women because of the smell," suggested Sarah.

"Well, funny that. I went to say goodbye to Ben and I'm now getting on rather well with the vet. Her name is Loretta."

"That's too many syllables, Jonathan. 'You must get her attention immediately!'"

"I call her Lori. That's one too many but it seems to work."

Sarah looked at her colleague. "I thought PC Preston was occupying your advances?" she asked.

"Emily," explained Jonathan, "she's rather clingy. I'll have to talk to her."

Sarah stared at the police dog handler. In truth they had an infrequent professional relationship and, while they fancied each other, it was from a distance. And yet, she felt close to this officer and was suffering with him. Which is why she had taken the action she had.

"You're in pieces, aren't you, mate?" she asked. "I think you need to get hold of things. Get back to being a dog handler."

"It's what I do best," he said. "I suppose I had better start looking for Ben's replacement." He paused. "Sarah, the thing that gets at me is that Watson deliberately killed Ben." He wiped his mouth.

"I know they are saying it was accidental but that doesn't help me."

Sarah frowned. "We'll never know. But it's not a good enough reason to waste all your training."

She now seemed distracted and was looking at some photographs she had taken out of her bag.

"Your baby daughter?" asked Jonathan.

She allowed her colleague to take the snapshots out of her hand. He stared at the pictures.

"German Shepherd?" he asked.

"It lived in a ground floor flat in Garden Square and was being badly treated: there were three squatters there – on drugs, of course – and a neighbour contacted the local authority who sent a dog warden."

Jonathan stared at the photographs.

"The louts claimed it was a stray," she added.

"So the dog warden took it away."

"They keep strays for a week to see if anyone claims them. The warden put the word out. I heard about it and went to see it."

Jonathan looked at the pictures again. "No, Sarah, it's too soon for me. I'm actually on two week's holiday. I'll face things when I get back to work."

She took the photographs from him. "There's only a day left. You could go and see it," she suggested.

"Has he got a name?" asked Jonathan.

"Lonely," laughed Sarah.

"Yes, he will be," sighed Jonathan.

"You're right, Jonathan," she announced, "It's the lovely vet and a prolonged period of self-pity for you." Sarah put her hand to her mouth. "Bugger," she said. "I've left my phone in the car and my husband will be chasing me. Just stay there, Jonathan."

She leapt up and ran the two hundred yards to the car park. She returned a few minutes later. She was cursing over the damage done to the back of her vehicle by the homeless dog which the warden had released into her temporary care. Jonathan was telephoning a veterinary practice in Stevenage. He yelled out in pain as the German Shepherd bit his ankle.

Within minutes he had taken the lead from Sarah, and he and the stray were running around the park together. They came back after eight minutes, breathless.

"Does he actually have a name?" he asked.

"Carlos," replied Sarah.

"I'm going to call him after you," he said.

"He's male, Jonathan, if you don't mind."

"Rud," he announced.

"Thanks," said Sarah. "I suppose I should be flattered."

He tied the lead to an arm of the bench and came round to face her.

"So it's back to work. Tell me that, Jonathan," she said.

"Yes. There's a long road ahead for Rud and me." He hesitated. "I think you're special, Sarah," he whispered.

He tried to kiss her but she turned her head.

"You know that we can't do that, Jonathan," she said.

He pulled away and released the dog. He slowly began to walk away. Sarah heard him repeat his name.

"Rud. Heel," he commanded as the German Shepherd disappeared into the woods.

"More's the pity," she said to herself, wiping her

lips.

+

The Duty Officer closed the cell door behind him and stared down at the prisoner. Harold Watson had his hands down his trousers.

"You won't hold me," he laughed. "I always get out. You lot can get stuffed." He pulled himself up and sat on the edge of the bed.

"You killed a police dog, Mr. Watson," said the police officer. "Have you any idea the distress that has caused its handler?"

"Fuck him," Watson snapped. "Should have held on to the vicious shit." He shuffled around on the mattress. "Anyway, it was bad luck. I was aiming at something else. He got his teeth into me and I fired in anger."

The Duty Officer looked carefully at the prisoner. He placed the breakfast tray on the table with some deliberation. "So, who were you aiming at, Mr. Watson?" he asked.

"Copper with the machine gun. I decided we'd go together, just like in 'High Noon'." He smiled and the police officer tensed. "I was Marshall Will Kane shooting the bad guy."

The Duty Officer stared at Harold Watson. "You wanted to kill a policeman?" he exclaimed.

"Fuckin' missed, didn't I," he snarled. "And you can't prove a thing, pal, so fuck off and leave me to enjoy my nosh."

The Duty Officer closed the cell door and went back to his desk to write a report to his sergeant.

+

Note. 'Suicide by Cop' is a recognised situation whereby a suicidal individual deliberately provokes their shooting by a police officer by adopting a threatening manner. There are two categories: first, as in this story, where the person who has decided to die at their own hands wants to be killed by a police officer, perhaps to act out their own fantasies. The second occurs when a cornered criminal, having committed a crime, decides to die rather than be arrested. This is achieved by using aggressive actions to convince the police that there is no other option but for them to shoot the felon. The term originated in the United States of America. It was first used in the United Kingdom by the Reverend Dr. William Dolman, who was a London coroner between 1993 and 2007. He set the legal precedent as a cause of death.

THE KEYS THAT DISAPPEARED - APRIL 2005

For the first time in her career, Detective Constable Sarah Rudd was unable to solve a crime. Sure, she had excuses aplenty: Marcus, now aged nearly five years old, was not settling down to his school work; Susie, despite a riotous first birthday party, was moody and apparently susceptible to infections; Nick, her husband, was stroppy, and money was not even tight – it was non-existent. And she was due to sit her sergeant's examinations. Sarah was also struggling in her conflict with the weighing scales. She was therefore relishing the prospect of a Saturday morning alone. The children were with the grandparents for the day and Nick was taking a group of pupils to the RAF museum at Hendon. She felt she was due a period of quality time alone and free of any stress. That was the dream. The reality was something rather different.

+

At ten fifteen on the morning of Saturday, 2 April 2005, Sarah closed the front door of her home and ignored the wave of her next door neighbour. Oliver and Alice Plumtree had moved into their house a few months earlier following the sale of their clothing business. Almost immediately he was undressing Sarah with his eyes. His crude comments were initially ignored: "Springtime is coming, Sarah. Time to get the bikini on."

On this one day he went too far for Sarah's liking. She had just been naked and standing on the scales in the bathroom. She found that if she shifted her stance to the left, she could reduce the digital result by two pounds. However, she was so desperate to achieve this lower reading that she toppled over and stubbed her toe. She was still suffering from the throbbing as she reached her car and heard a voice.

"Your buttocks are perfect for that skirt, Sarah."

She turned and stared at Oliver Plumtree. She strode over to the hedge and faced him. "You listen to me, you sad old man. I've spoken to you about this before. One more comment like that and I'll forget that I'm a lady." She paused and almost snarled at him, "You're sick, Oliver. You're a pervert."

He looked askance and almost stuttered his response. "I'm sixty-nine, Sarah. I'm only taking a healthy interest."

Sarah laughed, "Oliver, you can't remember was sex is. You're too old."

As she returned to her vehicle, his eyes lingered on her body. He spent the next hour reflecting on her words.

Sarah left the driveway and drove away rather too quickly. She reached the supermarket and spent the next forty minutes stretching the unused amount of credit on her bankcard in an effort to feed her family. She returned home, planning a long soak in the bath listening to U2. The lyrics reminded her that she needed her husband: *"Sometimes you can't make it on your own."*

She turned into the driveway and parked the car right up to the garage door so she could avoid her neighbour who she knew would rush out as soon as he spied her. She opened the boot lid and took out two shopping bags. She reached and opened the front door using both the keys required. She kicked the door ajar and carried the goods into the kitchen. She placed them on the floor. She returned to the car and collected the remaining three bags, which she carried into the house. She added them to the others in the kitchen and returned to the front door, which she closed. She followed her usual routine of taking her purse out of her pocket and putting it on the table. She then put her hand in her right hand coat pocket searching for the two sets of keys: one for the car and the other for the door. The front door keys were missing.

She opened the front door to check that they were not still in the lock. She riffled through her pockets and then went back to the kitchen and searched the worktop. She stood still and tried to recall all her movements since she arrived back home.

She had the keys when she opened the door. What did she do with them? She sometimes left them on the table by the entrance. The table top was clear. She usually put them in her pocket. She checked and re-checked and felt the lining. She went back to the kitchen. She had not unpacked the groceries. She left the bags alone. The whole area was visible and clear. She went back to the car and searched the driveway. She lifted the boot lid and checked the inside of the boot.

Sarah decided to return to the kitchen where, with great care, she unpacked the groceries, checking every single item and then the empty bags. She could not find the missing keys. She read a text message from Nick. She shuddered as she absorbed his words.

"This is all I fucking need," she said to herself

Following a cup of coffee, to which she added a measure of scotch to steady her nerves, her mind began to wander beyond normal limits.

Sarah decided to call the police. Twenty minutes later she answered the front door.

"Good morning madam. I'm Detective Constable Sarah Rudd. Can I come in?"

They went into the kitchen and sat down together.

"Now, madam, you've lost your front door keys. Take me through it from the beginning."

Sarah went through the morning's events in careful detail. The police officer took down copious notes and did not speak until she was sure the victim had completed her story.

"Right, madam. Just a few questions. Firstly, what is your usual routine when you enter your house?" She indicated that she did not want another cup of coffee.

"Well," stuttered Sarah. "I open the door with the two keys, I walk in and put down my bags, I put the keys on the hall table, I take out my purse and the car keys from my pockets, I take off my coat and then I go into the study when I keep my personal belongings. I put everything into my drawer."

"And this is what you did today?" asked DC Rudd.

"Er…" Sarah hesitated. "I opened the door and pushed it open. I went straight to the kitchen and put down the two shopping bags. I then…"

"Excuse me interrupting you, madam, but you must have done something with the keys. Did you put them on the table?"

Sarah searched her memory. "I may have slipped them into my pocket," she said.

"Could you have carried them into the kitchen?" asked the police officer.

"Well, I suppose I might have done. Let me think," said Sarah.

"Is it possible that you kept them in your hand and went back to the car, holding them?"

"I suppose… I went to the car and took out the three other bags of shopping and then I closed the rear door. Hang on," she exclaimed. "I had to take the car keys out of my pocket to lock the car. I could not have been holding the door keys at that point."

"That's good, Mrs. Rudd. Thanks," said DC Rudd. "Now we know that the keys were lost in between opening the front door and – when?"

"Right. When I went back to car I did not have them with me," said Sarah.

"So they were lost from when you opened the front door and carried your bags into the kitchen."

"Yes," exclaimed Sarah. "This is really helpful, Officer. They were either put on the hall table, or into my coat pocket, or I took them into the kitchen."

"Let's check the table first," suggested DC Rudd.

They went into the hall and searched everywhere. They lifted the table and looked underneath. There were no keys to be found.

"Let's check your coat, madam," said DC Rudd.

Sarah handed her the coat and the police office carefully checked each pocket. She then felt the internal linings. There were no keys evident.

"Madam, please stand still."

To her surprise, the detective then body-searched her, but said nothing.

"The keys must be in the kitchen," said DC Rudd.

"I discovered the loss before I unpacked the groceries," said Sarah.

The comment was ignored as they spent nearly fifteen minutes searching the whole room including the refrigerator and pantry. They sat down at the kitchen table and Sarah made them each a cup of coffee.

"What we'll do now, madam, is assume that you had the keys in your hand when you went back to collect the other bags and you dropped them on the way. You are sure that when you came to lock your car you did not have the door keys in your hand."

Sarah nodded and stood up. A few minutes later they were standing by her car, having searched the whole area. At the police officer's request, she unlocked the car and again searched the boot area.

Sarah shuddered as she realised that Oliver Plumtree had come through the gap in the hedge and was watching them. "Can I help?" he asked.

"You can go away," ordered Sarah, somewhat to the surprise of DC Rudd.

+

DC Rudd sighed. "Well madam, we've covered all the obvious possibilities. I suppose you've things on your mind?"

"Not really," said Sarah. "Just kids, husband, money and my weight."

DC Rudd laughed. "I've joined Weight Watchers. Put on a pound in the first week. Now madam, I think from what you are telling me that your usual practice is to open the front door and put the keys on the hall table."

"Yes," replied Sarah. "That's what I usually do."

"So," continued DC Rudd, "you unlocked the door, pushed it open, entered the hall, and put the keys on the table. You then went into the kitchen. Would the front door have been open all this time?"

Sarah's hand flew to her mouth. "I suppose it would have been but I was only gone for a few seconds," she cried.

"That's fine, madam. Let's just act it out."

They went back to the front door and into the porch area. Sarah unlocked the door, opened it, and went in. She put the spare set of keys she had taken from her drawer on to the table and went into the kitchen. She put down an imaginary bag of *groceries and walked out to the front door.*

"Madam," said DC Rudd, "you took eight seconds before you looked back at the door."

"So what?" snapped Sarah.

"Plenty of time for a sneak thief to have run in and stolen the keys."

"What are you talking about?" shouted Sarah. "Why would someone want my groceries?"

"It was your car they were after, madam. They thought you had put the car keys on the table. They have taken your door keys and, more likely than not, will have thrown them away."

"But... but we don't get sneak thieves in this area," exclaimed Sarah.

"Madam, they're everywhere, I promise you," said DC Rudd.

"But I'm a police officer. I would instinctively know if there was somebody in my house."

"What did you weigh in at this morning, madam?" asked the police officer.

Sarah groaned. DC Rudd was right. She had other things on her mind. She heard the front door closing as her visitor departed: she snapped out of her reverie.

As she regained a grip on the reality of her situation she waited nervously for Nick's arrival. He would be home in about two hours.

+

"You've bloody what!?" exclaimed Sarah as she absorbed the news that her husband had spoken to his parents and they had agreed to keep their children overnight. "Susie's going to hate it, Nick. What about her change of clothes? And she'll never sleep without her toys."

Nick growled as he tried hard to retain his composure. "You've lost our door keys. They could be in the hands of some nasty people who could be planning to visit us tonight."

Sarah slammed her foot on the ground. "I'm not telling you again, Nick. I would have sensed if someone had tried to take the keys while I was in the kitchen." She paused. "Nick, I'm a trained police officer."

He went to the front door and opened it. He placed a spare set of keys on the table. "I'll go and stand at the front gate," he said. "I'll run like Justin Gatlin and sneak the keys."

"Who's Justin Gatlin?" she laughed.

"American sprint champion. Ran the 100 meters in 9.88 seconds."

"Ha!" snorted Sarah. "You'll need to run faster than that to beat me."

Nick took up his position at the front gate, only to hold up his hand.

Sarah came out and saw that Oliver Plumtree had come through the side hedge and was speaking to Nick.

"Oliver. Go away," shouted Sarah.

"Hang on. He's trying to help us, Sarah," said Nick.

"No, he's not, Nick. He's taking any opportunity to leer at me."

Their neighbour retreated back to his own side and appeared to be muttering to himself.

"There's no need to take it out on an old man," chided her husband.

"Nick. He's a pervert. Right, back to our

positions," ordered Sarah.

She returned to the front door and indicated that she was ready. Nick shouted that she should retrace her steps to the kitchen, which she did. She pretended to place the imaginary shopping bags on the table and turned round. There was no one in sight.

She rushed to the front door and looked for Nick.

"Nick," she shouted. "Stop playing games. I'll do it again and this time will you please try to get the keys."

There was complete silence.

"Nick. I'm on the verge of getting rather angry," she shouted.

Her husband appeared from behind the car. He was waving a set of keys in his hand.

"Oh shit," cried Sarah as she burst into tears.

+

Having spoken to Marcus over the telephone and made mothering sounds for Susie, Sarah settled down on the lounge sofa and went over and over the events of the morning. She leaped up and retraced her steps. She yet again put her hands in her coat pockets and imagined finding the missing keys. She went outside and once more rejected the notion that an opportunist had sneaked in behind her back and snatched the keys.

Nick's mood was easing, helped by several cans of lager. His latest theory was that the keys had been stolen by a criminal hoping they fitted the car. When it was discovered they were front door keys they'd be sold on or thrown away. Sarah could not be bothered to inform him that DC Rudd had already considered that possibility.

He was becoming absorbed by the new hit from Mariah Carey:

"Who am I goona lean on
When times get rough
Who's goona talk to me
Till the sun comes up."

Finally they went to bed, having checked every window, catch and lock in the house.

Sarah pulled her husband to her and told him to stop giggling.

"This is crazy, Nick," said Sarah.

It was nearly midnight and Sarah again contacted the local police station to ask whether their keys had been handed in. She was angered by the negative response. They had barricaded the front door with tables and chairs but neither of them could sleep. They began to make silly excuses as to why one of them should get out of bed, ostensibly to make a cup of tea but, in truth, to review the security of the front door.

"This is madness, Sarah," said Nick as he jumped out of bed to peer through the bay window and look down at the front porch.

"Nick," said Sarah. She watched her husband turn to face her.

"Sorry," she whispered.

+

Nick arrived home the following afternoon and once again exploded with frustration. "£170 for a new lock!" he exclaimed. "We haven't got that sort of money."

"There was an emergency call-out fee, we have

two locks, and we need three spare keys," pleaded Sarah.

"It's absolutely ludicrous that you lost your keys, Sarah. You're a bloody detective. There must be an explanation."

"Nick, I've been over and over the events, which frankly were rather brief. If I'd mislaid them I would have found them. You proved to me that it could have been a nimble thief but we have an open front. I would have seen them. Oliver next door says he was cleaning his fishing equipment in the side shed and saw nothing. None of the other neighbours were interested. I can't recall seeing anyone in the street." She sighed, exhausted from a lack of sleep.

"Nick. We have new locks. Let's go and collect the kids. Your mum's been having problems with Susie."

"We move on," said Nick thrusting his arm around his wife. "Tell you what. I found been barricaded in last night quite arousing."

Later that night they wrapped themselves around each other. Sarah stroked her husband's hair.

"The case of the missing keys," suggested Nick.

"Well," sighed Sarah. "I guess that is one case that will never be solved."

+

Oliver Plumtree had parked and locked his car, and decided that he would try to walk round the lake three times, which would total six miles. He had left his wife Alice in bed complaining of a headache. This was her usual start to the day unless her arthritic pains were more dominating.

He had reached a point where he did not bother to

63

argue any more. He'd simply take her to the doctors and have the usual argument with the receptionists until they agreed that his wife would be given an appointment. He'd wait with her although she would not allow him to accompany her into the doctor's consulting room. She'd hand him the prescription. He'd take her home where she would position herself in front of the television and watch the daytime programmes. He would ask for a shopping list and then go to chemist and the supermarket, collecting the requisite pills and creams on the way back. He'd return back home and dispense the medicines before cooking Alice her lunch. She'd often go to bed in the afternoons, which was his opportunity to get some fresh air.

He looked across to the far side of the lake where the fishermen were occupying the allotted spaces. There was little wind to encourage the sailing folk.

He was slowly losing his self-respect. Sexual relations were a thing of the past for him and his wife. In fact, their last time together had been over a year ago and that had ended in her protesting that he had bruised her. He had resisted but, finally, he resorted to self-arousal. On each occasion he felt some relief but, at the same time, a sense of humiliation.

Oliver had started to fantasise over his nubile neighbour. He could not take his eyes off her full figure; and she wore such seductive outfits. Initially, she had seemed rather friendly, especially as he was building a relationship with Marcus. He began to wonder if she was finding him attractive. She had said, during their jokey chats, that she was frustrated by her husband's obsession with his work. On one occasion she had threaded her arm round his shoulders, and he had smelt her perfume. He decided

64

to test her appetite and began making gentle, innocent suggestions.

Sarah completely misread the situation and started to play up to him. This quickly came to an end when, on one occasion when they were alone in their gardens, he had called over to her and told her she'd look better without her bikini top.

Immediately Sarah retreated, dressed, and went back to see him. She left Oliver in no doubt that he was treading a dangerous path and it was stopping there and then. He was now entering a fantasy world and still believed that she had secret desires for him. However much she rebuffed him, his dreams continued.

Oliver stopped at the far end of the lake and sat down on one of the benches situated at the water's edge. He took out a nut roast bar and started to eat it.

"You shouldn't have said that, Sarah," he said to himself.

He stood up and spat out some of the nuts.

"Sick, am I," he snarled. "You bitch. Calling me a pervert."

He began to laugh to himself as he reflected on the antics of his neighbours over the last two days. He had watched Nick readying himself at the garden gate before dashing into the house and 'stealing' the keys. He had held back his merriment as he heard Sarah shout out, "Stop playing games."

He put his hand in his jacket pocket and took out a set of front door keys. He wound back his arm and threw them out into the deep water. They sank to the bottom and disappeared into the silt.

"Bitch," he repeated as he continued his walk round the lake.

+ + +

THE MYSTERIOUS CASE OF 'THE MOUSETRAP' - NOVEMBER 2005

Sarah Rudd was in a mean mood. She looked again at him. He was tall and elegant. The woman with him reminded her of husband Nick, which was not surprising as it was his mother. Sarah was worrying that she had failed her sergeant's examinations. Marcus was playing up and Susie was not sleeping. Their finances were in a mess. How much was tonight's celebration of her father-in-law's birthday costing? The meal at The Ivy was probably around one hundred and fifty pounds. The four seats in the Dress Circle at St. Martin's Theatre were forty pounds each: one hundred and sixty pounds. The taxi from the car park was dominated by a driver who was desperate to tell them who was the murderer. Why did Detective Constable Sarah Rudd want to see a stage play called 'The Mousetrap', which had been playing since 25 November 1952? She had read several of Agatha Christie's murder tales. She'd solved every one without trying. She looked at her husband as the curtain rose. He was dominated by his mother. Sarah decided that his chances of a romantic end to the evening were nil.

+

Sarah Rudd was elated.

"Did you see the notice in the foyer?" she exclaimed. "Tonight was the 20,621 performance of the show."

She threw her arms around her father-in-law and hugged him for all she was worth. They had found a hotel bar near to the theatre and were each fighting to establish their claim that they had solved the murder.

"Shush," ordered Nick's mother. "You know what

67

they said at the end of the play. We're to tell no-one what is the solution to the crime."

"Well, Mother. I solved it before the interval. It was obvious that…"

Nick put his hand over Sarah's mouth.

"Let's take a vote," said Mr. Rudd. "There were eight characters in the play. Who was our favourite?"

"I liked Christopher Wren," suggested Mrs. Rudd. "He was cuddly."

"Cuddly!" exclaimed her husband. "He was bonkers."

"Miss Casewell took my fancy," said Nick.

"She would," said Sarah. "She had a big bum."

Mr. and Mrs. Rudd senior stared at each other.

A second round of drinks and a bowl of peanuts were placed on their table. Mr. Rudd edged closer to his daughter-in-law, who had decided that he must have been a real flirt in his earlier days.

"Now tell me, Police Officer Rudd," he swooned. "What were the main clues that led to you solving the crime by the interval?"

Sarah gave the smile that disarmed men and made her husband feel seriously libidinous. "There was a massive one early on," she said. "Once I had worked out the significance of the possible cutting of the telephone line, I realised one person had the most to gain."

"I really did think that Mollie and Giles Ralston were so in love," said Mrs. Rudd. "They were brave, as well, to try to make a go of their guesthouse."

"I thought the stage setting was eerie," said Nick.

"You were meant to think that, Nicholas," interrupted his father.

Sarah froze to her chair. She hated it when they

68

called their son by his full name. She decided to take command of the proceedings. "It was a strange plot," she said. "A woman is murdered in London. A perfect couple, straight out of Evelyn Waugh, are opening their guesthouse. Five guests arrive: a potty architect, Mrs. Boyle, a dragon, who checks for dust on all the shelves, Major Metcalfe who seemed a relic from the Crimean War, Miss Casewell who, apart from seducing my husband, seemed totally out of place, and Mr. Paravicini who defied explanation. The radio is turned on and off so we learn about the murder in London and the fact that the south of England is snowed in. Mrs. Boyle is murdered but, as no one liked her, was this a diversion? Against all the odds, Detective Sergeant Trotter arrives on skis and says the police are expecting another murder."

The group discussion was ignited as each member wanted to comment. They dissected the second half of the play and re-visited the various clues. Sarah became progressively quieter, thinking to herself that they were all missing the obvious. She had known by the interval what the solution would most likely be.

They left the hotel, and Mr. Rudd hailed a taxi and directed the driver back to their car park. Mrs. Rudd would drive home, as a Christmas Day glass of sherry was her annual consumption of alcohol.

"Been to the show, folks?" asked the driver. He nodded as he received the confirmation he was expecting. "Worst kept secret in the West End," he laughed, "everybody knows it was..."

His prospective denouement of the murderer was interrupted by an Oriental bicycle rickshaw which was entertaining two unsuspecting American tourists with the night time sights of London. The cyclist was so busy pointing out the attractions in Leicester Square that he crossed in front of the cab and smashed into a headlight.

"You fucking Chinkie bastard!" the cabbie shouted.

+

Inspector Meredith groaned. He liked DC Rudd and he knew she had worked hard to pass her sergeant's examinations.

"Sarah," he said. "I can't create vacancies from nothing. We're fully staffed at the moment."

"I get that, sir, but Stevenage is hardly the centre of international crime."

"You played a part in the Harold Watson case," he suggested.

"That was awful," exclaimed Sarah. "The whole world knows he tried to kill a policeman. He told the Duty Officer just that."

"It was inadmissible, Sarah. The Duty Officer knew the rules. He was out of order to have that conversation with Watson in the cell." He sighed. "His brief made a fool of us in court."

"Since then, sir, I've arrested a man who was buying washing liquid, diluting it down, rebottling it, and making a fortune. And he gets off."

"What you need, DC Rudd, is a crime that requires pure detective work," suggested Inspector Meredith.

"In Stevenage, guv?"

+

Felicity Brown kissed her partner. He responded by

putting his hand up her back and making an attempt to undo her bra strap.

"Harry, we have loads to do," she laughed, as she went to kiss him. She pulled away.

"When are you going to ask me to marry you?" she asked.

"You might say no," answered Harry.

"I might at that."

"Have the builders left yet?" he asked.

"God, I hope so, Harry. This is the opening night of our restaurant and we're still building the kitchen." She realised that he had now undone the clasp of her bra.

"Harry. Is there time to go upstairs?"

"We have three tables and seven places booked," he said. "The first is arriving in twelve minutes time."

"We once managed it in six minutes," said Felicity recalling their carefree early times together.

"That was in Debenhams," he said.

He went outside and watched the torrential rain drench the canopy over the entrance to their restaurant. The neon lighting around 'The English Cuisine' was working well. The traffic in the centre of Stevenage was slowing by the minute. The flashing blue lights indicated the need for the emergency services to race to urgent callouts. The local radio station had already broadcast that the roof of an old people's home had collapsed and thirty-seven residents were being urgently re-housed. There were flashes of lightning, and all flights in and out of Luton airport were suspended.

The argument over the name of their establishment had raged over some weeks and eventually was settled by the exhaustion they each felt. It was not such a silly idea as it described exactly what they would be serving. The fact that their first dish of the day was Welsh lamb seemed irrelevant.

Harry went back inside and gasped. Felicity had changed into a pale green suit and looked stunning. She was talking to a man of average height who somehow had slipped in when Harry was distracted by events elsewhere.

"Harry," she said. "This is Mr. Binge. He's our first ever guest so I'm going to pour him a glass of champagne."

Mr. Binge held out his hand in Harry's direction. "Ronald," he said.

Harry hesitated as he accepted the contact.

"Let me save you the trouble," said their guest. "My parents had a funny sense of humour. They loved the British Force's Network music on the radio. You know: 'Elizabethan Serenade.' So they called me Ronald."

"Ronald Binge," repeated Harry. "But a co-incidence. Not the composer." He looked around him.

"I'm a music teacher," he said. "I'm staying here in Stevenage tonight. I'm examining some school children in the morning." He accepted the glass of bubbly and allowed Felicity to show him to his table. She nodded as he asked for a beer, and she handed him a menu.

Harry turned round and realised that two more diners were arriving.

As they attempted to drain off the rain from their coats and shake their umbrellas, they still found time to carry on their argument.

"This is ridiculous," said the woman. "I could have

72

found a babysitter. We didn't need your mother."

"She's free," replied the harassed listener.

"With your mother, there's always a price to pay," she said.

Harry managed to gain their attention and directed them to a secluded table in the window bay. As they sat down he hesitated.

"Excuse me, but we've met before. Aren't you..."

Sarah stood up and held out her hand. "Detective Constable Sarah Rudd and this is my husband, Nick."

Harry nodded towards the downtrodden partner.

"We met, Mr. Howard, several weeks ago when I was trying to trace some diluted washing up liquid. You were helpful. Thanks. Anyway I'm off-duty tonight so if there are cockroaches in the rice, don't worry."

Harry chuckled. "Is it a co-incidence that you're with us tonight?" he asked.

"Nope," said Sarah. "I sneaked a look at your menu. I'm going to have the Shepherd's pie."

"Am I allowed to offer you a complementary glass of champagne?" asked Harry.

"Sadly not. Everything on the bill, please," said Sarah.

As the owner wandered off to fetch the drinks, Nick glared at his wife. He pushed his hand through his hair, which was usually a sign he was winding up to launch a verbal assault.

"Don't go there," anticipated Sarah. "I know it's political correctness gone mad but we have to be so careful. Supposing there was a fight in here and the squad car boys come?" Sarah sighed. "Anyway, I want to talk about our sex life."

Nick groaned. "That should be a brief

conversation," he said.

"Exactly," said Sarah. Her thoughts wandered back to her family, and Nick's mother who was babysitting for them.

Despite the distractions, they settled down to read the menu and watched as the waiter poured them both a glass of wine, which neither of them had ordered.

Behind the scenes, the chef had convinced Harry that all was organised, and they checked the vegetables. He was concerned over the decision to offer cauliflower with a grilled cheese topping. The lamb and turkey were roasting perfectly. Harry allowed himself a small glass of Chablis. Things were going rather well, and he was unable to prevent himself anticipating the sight of Felicity undressing out of her green outfit after all their satisfied guests had left.

Felicity knew it was Mrs. Craven who had walked through the door. She had been difficult when she prefaced her reservation on their website by demanding to know what vegetables would be available and how they were being prepared. She was soaked to the skin, and responded angrily when Felicity tried to direct her into the ladies' cloakroom. She eventually was shown to a table next to Ronald Binge. She sighed and straightened the knives and forks. She held the salt cellar upside down and shook it.

"It's empty," she advised Felicity, who took it from her, turned the base, and then brushed away the resulting shower of condiment.

Harry was directing the waitress and watching as Colonel Wainwright arrived, shaking off the rain from his trench coat.

"Hell's bells," cried the military man, "might as well be back in The Falklands."

At that moment, Harry remembered that the generator had not been commissioned into service. He decided it would take more than heavy rain to spoil their opening night. He looked across their restaurant and spotted Felicity chatting away to Mr. and Mrs. Rudd. She was bending forward, and Harry could not help having nocturnal thoughts. He also thought the police officer was attractive. She had a full figure and carried it well.

Ella Packer was completely comfortable and dry as she entered The English Cuisine. She was seated almost immediately and seemed oblivious to Harry's charm.

Harry pressed himself on Felicity, and whispered into her ear, "Six here, one to come."

"We've had a cancellation," she replied.

At that exact moment, there was an explosion of thunder across the skies, and the entire building shook. The lights went out. All conversation in the restaurant stopped.

"Get the generator going," shouted the Colonel.

+

During the three hours from five o'clock that afternoon, it was calculated that over two inches of rain fell on the Stevenage area. The emergency services were overwhelmed. Felicity was in her element. She sent all the staff home, suggested to her guests that they all sit round one table, which was created by moving various parts of the furniture.

Harry lubricated the arrangements by providing various wines, which he placed down the centre of the festivities amongst the candles providing light and atmosphere. Each guest received a pre-prepared plate of hors d'oeuvres, and Felicity explained that there was enough heat left in the ovens for her to serve a dish of roast lamb, vegetables, and mashed potato.

"Here's to the success of The English Cuisine," proposed the Colonel.

Everyone raised their glasses, except for Mrs. Craven who was poking around her plate.

"Are these prawns defrosted?" she asked.

Nick Rudd was sitting between the Colonel and Ella Packer, and was beginning to enjoy himself. Sarah was the other side of the Colonel with Harry on her right-hand side. Mrs. Craven was beginning to converse with Ronald Binge.

"So, how long have you two been married?" the Colonel asked Felicity who was opposite him.

"We're not married," replied Harry. "We're partners."

""You've changed your name then, Felicity," said Ella Packer.

"I can't keep up with all this modern stuff," said Mrs. Craven. "Living together, changing names without getting married. Two people should go to the altar, take the vows, and keep to them."

"But married couples lie to each other all the time," said Harry.

"I was born Felicity Brown," said Felicity. Several heads turned towards her.

"I was born Henry Brown," said Harry. "It's a coincidence. We have common surnames." He looked across the table. "Don't you agree, Nick?

Couples lie to each other."

Nick gave the question some thought. He was aware that Ella had turned to face him. She had been picking at her food and discarded most of the items on her plate.

"Two people don't lie deliberately. It's usually because they want to live in harmony and not offend the other party. If your wife says, "Did you enjoy my Shepherd's Pie?" and, as it happens, you didn't, you might reply, "It had some wonderful flavourings!" and not say, "It was bland and tasteless.""

"But if a man is having an affair, he will lie," said Ella Packer. "Mine did, and my solicitor says it will cost him hundreds of thousands of pounds."

"Well, Nick, you have to tell the truth," said Felicity.

"Why is Nick so virtuous?" asked Mrs. Craven.

"His wife is a detective," Felicity announced. "We have Detective Constable Rudd with us."

"I'm off duty," said Sarah, and drank some more wine.

"Sarah is a wife, mother, cook, and best friend, and then a police officer," said Nick.

"Am I?" said Sarah as she pondered her husband's interpretation of her roles in life.

"Music is the most truthful form of human contact," said Ronald Binge. "Is there a more emotional piece than Tchaikovsky's Overture to Romeo and Juliet?"

"West Side Story for me," said Ella. "When Anita sings 'One Hand, One Heart' I just go to jelly. We had that for our wedding service."

"No wonder you are divorcing, dear. You're living in a fantasy world" said Mrs. Craven.

"Fuck you," snarled Ella. "I'm screwing the shit out of him for what he did to me."

"Sounds like there was a lot of screwing in your marriage," said the Colonel.

+

Felicity and Harry started to clear the first course plates just as the electricity came back on. The guests had a chat, and decided they would prefer to finish the meal by candlelight. The Colonel surprised everyone by announcing he would pay for the whole evening. Nick looked at Sarah who nodded in agreement. The rain was abating, and Harry reported that traffic was beginning to flow more freely. Felicity asked for ten minutes to prepare the roast lamb.

Mrs Craven and the Colonel were seen disappearing into a corner of The English Cuisine. Harry alternated between serving drinks and trying to get as close to Sarah as he could. Ella was giving Nick the full version of her marriage, including the bedroom romps. Ronald Binge was reviewing the selection of CDs located by the sound system. The sense of anticipation grew as their dinner neared.

The lights went on, and Ronald Binge cried out, "No, no. That ruins the atmosphere. I have the music of Mahler here to play."

Felicity stood with her arms folded. "Someone has taken the cash from the till," she said.

"How much?" asked Sarah.

"That's not the point," said Felicity. "Anyway, you're the bloody detective. You solve it."

"A few pounds is my guess," said Sarah. "I'm off duty. Do you want to call the police?"

"Absolutely not," said Harry. "When are you serving the lamb, darling?"

"I'm not. The evening is over as far as I am concerned," said Felicity.

"Felicity!" sighed Harry. "You can't do that."

"I have a suggestion to make," said Sarah. "Turn the lights off and let's have one final drink together."

There seemed to be a collective sigh of relief as the guests responded to the darkened atmosphere and the opening bars of Mahler's Resurrection Symphony. For about fifteen minutes, they mingled and talked. Then the lights were switched back on.

"I think I'd like to go upstairs," said Felicity.

Harry decided that perhaps the evening was not a complete disaster. An angry Felicity was to be relished.

"You might want to look in your till, Felicity," said Sarah.

Felicity looked puzzled, but went to the reception desk, and checked the cash drawer. "It's here, the cash," she yelled. "I promise you it was missing. I'm so pleased. Thank you."

The guests left the restaurant as the Colonel announced he'd had a lot of fun. Mrs. Craven said she thought the cutlery needing polishing. Ella tried to give Nick her phone number. Ronald Binge left last, still absorbed by the music.

+

As they sat back in their taxi, Nick asked Sarah what had happened.

"It was the case of the Mousetrap," she answered.

"What's that to do with it? Someone took the cash

and then put it back."

"Not quite. Yes, one of the people in the room took the cash. Not difficult as the code to the till is on a piece of paper on Felicity's desk. I knew who it was. I suggested they put it back. They did. End of story." She sighed suggestively. "I've enjoyed the evening, Nick."

"Mousetrap? What are you talking about?"

"What was the ending to the play, Nick? Somebody wasn't who the audience thought they were." She kissed her husband. "If you remember, I had solved the riddle by the interval. Even your father was impressed."

"So you're saying that someone tonight wasn't kosher."

"There was an opportunist amongst us," said Sarah.

"So who?" demanded Nick

Sarah leaned over and again kissed her husband, allowing her hand to wander. "Anita didn't sing 'One Hand, One Heart' in West Side Story, Nick. It was sung by Tony and Maria." Sarah chuckled. "If you had spent more time looking at Ella Packer's unblemished fingers instead of trying to see the size of her bum, you'd have noticed that she's never worn a wedding ring."

"So you suggested that she put the cash back," said Nick.

"She told me to fuck off. I suggested she might like to spend the rest of the evening with some large friends of mine. She said that I had said I was off duty. I told her I am always a police officer."

"You didn't like what I said, did you, Sarah?"

"About being a wife, mother, chief bottle washer,

and then a police officer? I understand where you were coming from, Nick."

"Sarah," said Nick. "Is it okay? Me having this thing about women and big bums."

Sarah squeezed a personal part of his anatomy as the taxi driver slowed his vehicle and Sarah prepared to greet Nick's mother who would want to tell them everything their children had been doing.

"It's very okay, Nick. I stood on the scales this morning. I think all your fantasies will come true tonight."

Two weeks later, Sarah's own dreams came true when she was told she had passed her examinations. However, she would have to wait a little longer before a sergeant's job became available.

+ + +

A MATTER OF TIME - FEBRUARY 2006

Inspector Meredith groaned as he waited for her response.

"But, sir. I'm a sergeant now. I'm ready for increased responsibilities." Sarah Rudd was warming to her task. "I've worked hard for my promotion."

"Sarah," sighed the Inspector, "you must wait for a vacancy." He offered her an avuncular smile. "You'll have to be patient." He closed the file in front of him. "That's something you don't relish, isn't it?

"Guv," stated Sarah, "my promotion belongs to me, my husband, and my children. I'm in a hurry for them."

Inspector Meredith stared at one of his favourite officers. "Sarah," he said, "it's only a matter of time."

+

Detective Constable Sarah Rudd stared across the desk. She had not taken to Detective Sergeant Jeremy Smith from day one, which was twelve weeks ago. If it were not for the fact that Sarah was about to become Sergeant Rudd, their antipathy would have developed into open warfare. Sarah suspected he was on the inside track – public school and the rest. The rumours from Croydon, from where he had come, told of his ambition, talent, and libido.

"Get someone else," argued DC Rudd. "I'm not reviewing a case that another officer has fucked up. End of story."

"You are doing just that," ordered DS Smith. He picked up the file in front of him and handed it to Sarah. "DS Trimble has been seconded to the Met, and DC Tanner is on sick leave."

Sarah snatched at the file. "Why was DC Tanner given this case in the first place, Guv? He's a weak officer; we all know that," she said.

DS Smith was aware of that assessment, but was not willing to confide his view that DS Trimble had his mind on other events. "I'll not have comments of that nature made in this office, DC Rudd," he replied. "In fact, DC Tanner had been to Winderfield School several times to investigate the theft of some bikes by the locals."

Sarah left the office in a huff. A few minutes later, as she entered the canteen for her coffee break, she sighed with pleasure. She grabbed her cup and went over to a table where an officer was reading a daily paper.

"Forty-two teeth! That's what you said," she exclaimed.

PC Jonathan Robinson looked up, smiled and stood up. "The one and only Sarah Rudd," he said, before hugging her. "Congrats on the exams."

"You've heard," said Sarah, as she tried to get some air into her lungs. They sat down together.

"How's Rud?" asked Sarah.

"He's become a specialist in pub fights. He's ferocious."

They laughed together, and their eyes met. They had last seen each other eight months ago, but their flirtation was as strong as ever.

"What's this about forty-two teeth?" asked Jonathan.

"You said that Rud has that number," she replied.

"That was Ben. Rud has about thirty-six because a thug kicked him in the mouth."

"Ugh! What happened?" asked Sarah.

"The thug lost the fight," said Jonathan. They looked at each other.

"Well, thirty-six teeth will be fine," said Sarah. "I want you and Rud to hide outside DS Smith's office and, when he bends over, I want Rud to bite him as deeply as possible in his rear."

"Do I get the impression there is some antipathy here?" commented Jonathan.

"He's making me review a case. Some schoolgirl making false claims. DC Tanner fucked up on the case. He goes on sick leave, his boss goes to the Met, and DC Rudd has to ride to the rescue."

"I hope you're not pre-judging the situation," said Jonathan.

"Then you bloody solve it," flared Sarah.

"Me and Rud have a bum to bite," laughed Jonathan.

+

DC Sarah Rudd sat at her desk and reviewed the case of Lucy Maybank.

In November 2005, early on a Wednesday afternoon at around 2.25pm, in the changing rooms of Winderfield Private School for girls on the north side of Stevenage, a teenager was discovered by a teacher in an individual shower cubicle, following lunchtime athletics practice. Her tracksuit bottoms were around her ankles and her two pairs of knickers were down to her thighs. A later medical examination confirmed that she had engaged in sexual intercourse. The male had used a condom.

Lucy Maybank initially said that intercourse had

not taken place and she had been arousing herself with a dildo. This was never located. Lucy was fifteen years, eleven months old. Her parents, both civil servants, immediately caused tension by accusing the school of a lack of security. Lucy then changed her story and said that consensual sex had taken place. She refused to reveal the other party.

A team, led by DC Tanner, who reported to DS Trimble, had conducted exhaustive enquiries. These, in themselves, were inconclusive. Lucy was sexually well advanced and was known as a 'teaser''. She had made life difficult for two of her male teachers. On the day in question, there were few people around at the suspected time the incident took place. Other girls had come and gone. Lucy was a loner who had few close friends although she was generally popular. She had left the running track at 1.45pm, an event recorded by Heather Brown, the PE teacher. She was found forty minutes later in the showers.

The police investigations centred on three males, all of whom were in the area and could have perpetrated the offence: sexual intercourse with an under-age person. There was a shadowy fourth person who had been seen briefly by two of the suspects. Lucy stuck to her story, her parents decided to concentrate on their coming divorce, and DC Tanner went to the doctor claiming stress. The file had been passed to DS Jeremy Smith.

DC Sarah Rudd read the report twice, making brief notes on the second occasion.

"Why?" she said to herself. "Why Lucy or Lucee?"

+

DC Sarah Rudd looked at the head teacher with a certain sympathy. Her husband Nick provided her with graphic stories of the challenges of running a school in the modern world of sexual maturity, internet and social media influences, and parents who sued for the lamest of reasons.

"Thank you for coming to see me, Officer Rudd," said Malcolm Williams, "but we think the matter is closed. Lucy says it is was consensual, and her parents do not wish us to pursue the matter."

"We don't agree with that, Mr. Williams," replied DC Rudd. "By her own admission, Lucy Maybank had sexual relations. She was under sixteen years of age at the time. The other party may be guilty of an offence. My job is to find out the facts. You called us to your school. The girl's parents contacted us. My colleague DC Tanner conducted a thorough investigation. I'm here to complete his work."

"Why you? We have not seen DC Tanner for several weeks," said the head teacher. He paused. "Surely the police have more important cases to investigate?"

Sarah ignored his comments. "I'll start today by meeting with Royston Hibbert," she said.

The Interview with Royston Hibbert

From the start, Sarah didn't like Royston Hibbert. He asked if he could smoke, and pulled a face at the answer he received. He then objected to being referred to as a groundsman. He was 'Head Groundsman,' he claimed.

"Mr. Hibbert. According to the statement you have made, you were cutting the grass during the lunch period when Lucy Maybank was assaulted."

Sarah Rudd hesitated. "Does grass grow in November?"

"All year round. Milder winters. Anyway, she weren't," sneered Hibbert. "She's a saucy one. She fucked one of the teachers, and it went wrong."

"The area you were working in," continued Sarah, "backs onto the shower rooms. Your petrol-powered lawnmower was, according to several witnesses, not heard after two o'clock. You are unable to explain where you were. You were seen again at about two forty-five, running to your car. You drove away at high speed." She thought carefully. "Mr. Hibbert, please understand that we consider you a prime suspect."

"Wasting your time, copper," said Hibbert. "You've no witnesses. Lucy won't say who it was."

Sarah interrupted him, "So you've spoken to Lucy about this, have you?"

"Everybody knows. There's no secrets here."

"Which is exactly your problem, Mr. Hibbert," Sarah paused. "If I have to interview every single pupil and teacher at this school, I will. I'll find someone who will place you near to, or in, the showers. So why don't you save yourself a lot of bother and tell me the truth." Sarah paused again. "And take your hands out of your pockets, sit up straight, and stop wasting my time."

"Weren't me," said Royston Hibbert.

"So where were you, Mr. Hibbert, on that day between two and two-thirty?"

"I was on my way to the doctors," he said.

"Why. What was wrong with you?" asked Sarah.

"I had split my foreskin. I needed help."

"Pardon?" asked Sarah.

"Look. I'm surrounded by these girls all day long. Have a look at them. They're fucking hot and they know how to use it. I know the penalties. I'm not fucking stupid and I need this job."

"I'm not following this, Mr. Hibbert," said Sarah.

"I get randy. So when it gets too much, I go to my shed. It's my private area."

"For what reason?"

"To have a wank. Are you stupid? What else would I do?"

"So why did you go to the doctors?"

Royston Hibbert dropped his head into his hands. "My fucking foreskin split, didn't it. It was agony."

"So all I have to do is to interview your doctor who will confirm all this?"

Royston looked at the police officer. "Yes and no," he said.

"Royston. Stop playing games with me," snapped Sarah.

"I went to the doctors, yes."

"Thank you, Mr. Hibbert," she sighed.

"But not till the next morning."

"Why? You were in pain."

"I was fucking embarrassed. I went home but it was all swollen so I got an appointment the next morning."

"So what did the doctor say?" asked Sarah.

"Got to be circumcised. Go in next week. Bloody waiting list." Royston paused. "Would you like to see it?"

"Your foreskin could have split while you were having relations with Lucy," said Sarah.

Royston Hibbert laughed. "She'd have told the whole school," he said.

"Mr. Hibbert, have you ever had sex with Lucy Maybank?" asked Sarah.

Royston Hibbert stood up and put a cigarette in his mouth. "Somebody did, copper," he said. "Weren't me," he added as he walked out of the interview.

+

The Interview with Jaroslaw Michalski

The early part of the interview was clear enough. Music teacher Michalski had been organising a concert evening for the pupil's parents, which took place two weeks after the Lucy Maybank incident. The case notes revealed that Lucy was a talented flautist. She had arranged to meet the music teacher at two forty-five in the afternoon in his room on the day of the incident. The music centre where Michalski was based was adjacent to the changing rooms. This was a sensible arrangement as it allowed the playing of instruments during the day without disturbing lessons elsewhere. DC Tanner had written down that Lucy was working with Mr. Michalski on her rendition of the flute solo in Malcolm Arnold's 'Fantasy'.

Sarah stared at the nervous man in front of her. "Mr. Michalski, you know why I am here?"

"Yes. Because of what happened to Lucy," he said.

"I read here that you were next door to the changing rooms in your office. You were expecting Lucy to arrive for her music lesson. There was a sudden commotion involving staff and police, and you heard nothing?"

"I heard nothing. That is correct," said Michalski.

"Your English is very good," said Sarah.

"I came here when I was six. You hear I still have my Polish accent."

"So you heard nothing?" Sarah repeated.

"I had my headphones on. We have expensive equipment in the music room. The school is good to me. I was listening to a new recording of Chopin's piano pieces. That is my instrument. The piano. There is nothing to compare with Chopin's etudes. I was lost in his music. I began to wonder where Lucy was. I took off my headphones and then a boy came into my room and told me there were police in the building. I went next door and saw Lucy being led away. A policeman took a statement from me. I was later interviewed by Mr Tanner."

"Detective Constable Tanner," said Sarah.

"Yes. I spent nearly an hour with him."

"I have read his notes," said Sarah. "The truth is, Mr. Michalski, that you had enough time to go into the changing rooms, meet with Lucy, and then go back and listen to Chopin."

"That is true," said Jaroslaw.

"You must get close to your students," said Sarah. "Especially some like Lucy, who I understand is very talented."

"We have some wonderful musicians here," said Michalski. "But only a few, perhaps two or maybe three, have the ability to do more than play the music."

"I don't understand that," said Sarah.

"The notes are the notes. That is why they practise so hard. To make sure they play the right notes as the music is written."

"So what is different about Lucy?" asked Sarah.

"She does not see notes. She feels music. She has the wonderful ability to try to understand what the composer was trying to say." He drank some water. "She believes she can become a world class flautist. She has even thought of changing her name to Lucee. She thinks it has a more classical tone to it." He laughed. "I've not told anybody about that."

"You make it sound as though she plays in a kind of fantasy world."

"We are playing with words… er… Mrs…. police…"

"Detective Constable Rudd," said Sarah.

"Yes. Detective Constable Rudd. You are not a music lover."

"James Blunt. Eminem. Coldplay," said Sarah.

"As I say, you are not familiar with proper music," he said. He looked at her. "Detective Constable Rudd. Let's stop playing games with each other. You have no idea who Lucy was with on that day and you never will. Schools are closed societies. We keep to ourselves. Lucy does not want it known who she was with and so you'll never find out. Now why don't we make your day more pleasant? Come down to my room and I'll play you some Chopin."

But Detective Constable Sarah Rudd was ninety-nine per cent sure that she already knew who had been in the showers with Lucy on that day.

+

Interview with Hugo Sloane-Wrighton
"You're not wearing a uniform. How disappointing."

DC Rudd looked up at the individual who had just walked into the room.

"I love women dressed in outfits," he continued.

"Please sit down. Mr. Sloane-Wrighton, I assume." Sarah stood up. "I'm a detective," she said. "We don't wear uniforms and that will be the last personal comment you make. Do we understand each other, Mr. Sloane-Wrighton?"

"Ouch. It's Hugo." He sat down and smiled.

"Mr. Sloane-Wrighton. You found Lucy in the showers."

"A girl called me in to help. I was having a break and a ciggie. We called the police and an ambulance. Lucy was taken away quite quickly."

"You were interviewed by DC Tanner, and you could not explain where you had been for the previous thirty minutes." Sarah continued to look down at the file in front of her.

"I was able to say exactly where I had been. I walked around the playing fields. I had something on my mind. What I could not do was provide any evidence because I did not see anybody. We have extensive recreational acres here, DC Rudd. If you want to be alone, it's not difficult."

Sarah Rudd rifled through the pages of the file. "You did not say why you wanted to be on your own," she said.

"I was not asked the question," replied Hugo.

"Why did you want to be on your own?" asked Sarah.

"Because, Detective Rudd, I had received a letter that morning in the post telling me I had not even been given an interview for the position of Head of English at Stow School."

Sarah continued to review the notes in front of her. "The post must arrive early in your area," she said.

"My partner texted me. She had opened the letter."

"What time was that?" asked Sarah.

"At exactly 12.30pm. I was on dinner duty. I asked a colleague to cover for me and I went for a walk." He paused. "I am keen to get away from this place."

"That's rather convenient, isn't it? DC Tanner has recorded the fact that you talk about the girls in a rather patronising way. Where were you educated, Mr. Sloane-Wrighton?"

"Eton, and Trinity, Oxford."

"I find it rather strange that in the middle of a busy school day you managed to disappear for so long," said Sarah.

"Detective Rudd. Do you really think I would allow myself to become involved with any of the girls here? You obviously don't like me. But I can assure you that finding lovely women is not an issue for me."

Sarah looked at the English master. "No," she thought to herself, "I don't suppose it is."

+

Her knock at the front door was answered almost immediately.

"Mrs. Tanner," said Sarah. "I'm Detective Constable Sarah Rudd. I'm a colleague of your husband. May I come in, please?"

The thin, quite pretty woman remained silent as she showed the visitor into the front room of the semi-detached house.

"Dave said you would be calling," she said as she opened the door. "I'll make some tea."

Sarah walked in and found David Tanner. He was unshaven, and seemed nervous. He held out his hand, inviting Sarah to sit down.

"How are you, David?" Sarah asked.

"I heard you were reviewing the Lucy Maybank case," he said. "So I told Jane you'd be calling." He stood up and went over to the table and picked up an envelope. It was marked 'Confidential. DC Rudd'. He handed it to his visitor. "It's all in there. You're DC Sarah Rudd. I knew immediately that you would work it out."

"Why, Dave. Why throw your career away?" asked Sarah.

"I'm asking myself the same question, Sarah." He wiped his eyes. "Jane is pregnant."

"What happened to you?" she asked.

"I went to the school to investigate the theft of some bicycles. One of them belonged to Lucy. I managed to locate it and took it round to her house. She was on her own. I had no idea she was under sixteen. I could not help myself. She invited me in and gave me a drink. She played some hypnotic music on her CD player. It was crazy. We went upstairs. She stripped off her clothes very slowly. She then lay on the bed and spoke in a quiet tone but she made it clear what she wanted.

"I met her at the school in the grounds perhaps three times. On the day in question, she was funny and said we were finished. I watched her complete her athletics practice, and I followed her into the showers. We had sex, and then she went into a huff. She started moaning. I heard someone in the room but I managed to escape. For some reason she did not name me. Then DS Trimble told me I had to take the case over. I tried to get out of it but his mind was on the Met move. I went through the motions but it was all too much. I saw my doctor and he immediately signed me off."

Sarah stood up as his wife came into the room with a tray of tea.

"I have to go. Sorry," said Sarah.

"I've told Jane everything," he said. His wife looked at Sarah with pleading eyes.

"Just one thing, Sarah," said David.

Sarah paused and turned back.

"How did you work it out?" he asked.

"It's one of the worst files I've ever read. There was no intention of solving the case."

"Just that?" asked David Tanner.

"Try 'Lucy' and 'Lucee'," said Sarah. "I realised you had been on intimate terms with Lucy for her to tell you about her proposed change of name."

"She played the flute for me," said David as he moved towards his wife.

"She played you for the fool," thought Sarah as she left their house.

+

Detective Sergeant Jeremy Smith had finished reading DC Rudd's report, and was now scanning the letter from DC Tanner.

"What a shame," he said. "He's a good detective. I suppose we'll have to follow procedure."

"You suppose what!" exclaimed Sarah. "He's a married man and he had sex with an underage girl. Throw the book at him."

DS Smith looked over his glasses and stared at

Sarah. "What right have you to be so moralising," he said. "These girls try it on all the time. DC Tanner was a little silly, I agree."

Sarah stood up. "Now you listen to me. I expect you to adhere to protocol. We don't judge. We have a procedure which we always follow."

Sarah left the room and turned right down the corridor.

"Sarah," shouted a voice.

"What?" she yelled. She turned round to face Inspector Meredith.

"Are you alright, Sergeant Rudd?" he asked.

"I'm fine, sir. I'm sorry. Just a disagreement with another officer."

He laughed. "You mean with DS Smith?"

"Yes, Guv. I'll have to apologise."

"Well, perhaps."

Sarah stood very still. "Guv, what did you call me?"

"Sergeant Sarah Rudd," he replied. Your promotion and move are now official."

Sarah went weak at the knees.

Inspector Meredith held out his hand. "I hear you've just sorted out a difficult case," he said. "Walking the streets will be a relief." He smiled. "Good luck, Sarah." He turned to move away down the corridor and then turned back. "Sarah," he said. "As a police officer there is only ever one decision. That is the right decision." He paused. "I think your last case told you that."

Sarah moved on past DS Smith's office door. She made her way to the canteen where she purchased a coffee. She sat down at a table and texted her husband and her parents.

"Room for a good-looking police officer?"

She looked up and saw Jonathan. She stood up and threw her arms around him.

"All my dreams are coming true," he said.

Sarah told him her news.

"Don't forget, me and Rud are the answer to the pub fights," he laughed. His hand went up to his mouth. "Hell, Sarah. I'm so sorry. We've not had time to bite the bum you had selected."

Sarah looked at Jonathan. "DS Smith is history," she said. "Sergeant Sarah Rudd is in town."

"And God help the bad guys," said her friend.

+ + +

A GAME OF TWO HALVES - OCTOBER 2006

He was driving recklessly but the match started at 10.30am and he never let his son down. He sped down the Bowditch Road straight through the traffic speed control cameras. There were two flashes and he laughed. "ANPR for a laugh," he said to himself as he swerved to avoid a cyclist. "Stands for 'Absolutely No Prosecution Resulting'." He had thought that up himself. He sped on. He was never late for his son.

+

Sergeant Sarah Rudd was off duty. The early months as a Community Officer dealing with integration of the ethnic minorities in the inner areas of Stevenage were proving both exacting and fulfilling. She had bonded her team together and established links with the key agencies. Two of her constables were working effectively within the school communities. Sarah was a natural leader, and her disarming of an agitated Asian shop-keeper who had been robbed three weeks' running and who was proposing to mutilate a child shoplifter with a cleaver, merely added to her growing reputation.

She looked around as she waited to collect Susie from play school. She and Nick had agreed that the extra expenditure was necessary, and a credit card offer, giving them a fifteen months' interest-free period, solved the short-term financial problem. They were comforted by the continued strength of the British economy and a Chancellor of the Exchequer who had announced that the era of boom and bust was over. Their son, Marcus, now five and a half years old, was happy at school; their own parents were coping with the challenges of geriatric decline. Overall, Sarah was content. The extra pay that came with promotion had made a difference.

She sighed as she reviewed the bill she had paid earlier in the day for some clothing. How could she deny him? Marcus was into football and every time they were out together, albeit infrequently, she had a mild panic when they spotted lads wearing Chelsea shirts. They had won the 2005/06 Premier league by 91 points against a tally of 83 points from their nearest rival. What mattered was that it was Manchester United whose shirt Marcus was wearing with pride. Even Susie was with them when they had watched England lose on penalties to Portugal in the quarter-finals of the Football World Cup.

Life was good for Sergeant Sarah Rudd. They always found a way around their financial challenges, and Nick's prospects as a teacher were improving as he showed more ambition. Although many years ahead, they could both anticipate receiving decent pensions. They had already had one, alcohol-fuelled, daydream about moving to live in Spain. They never spoke about it but there were also two inheritances coming their way, one day in the future. Nick would have to share with his sister who he never spoke either to or about. Beyond all else they had Marcus and Susie.

For Sarah, there was just the one, on-going, conundrum in her life. She had stood on the scales that morning and followed her usual, slightly comical, practice of moving her feet around the surface in an attempt to reduce the reading by half a pound. The

100

digital volcano was unwavering: she was eleven stone and half a pound. She went back into the toilet and strained in an attempt to persuade her bladder to release a few more drops of urine. She heard the sound she was praying for and rushed back to the bathroom. Eleven stone and half a pound. On one occasion she had cut her nails to see if that helped the weight reduction she was desperately seeking.

Her physiology was strong. She carried herself with real presence and the police uniform had, for her, added to the personal allure. She did not really feel overweight, whatever the weight tables proclaimed – just uncomfortable. She had recently studied them. With the best will in the world she could not claim to have a 'small frame'. She was five foot, seven inches tall and the parameters of 123 to 136 did not apply to her. She was of a 'medium frame' build and so she needed to register between 133 and 147 pounds meaning her weight should be ten stone, five pounds. She decided that this was ridiculous and she was really a small, 'large frame'. At last she was within the limits: 143 – 163. Her joy at being 154 and a half pounds against eleven stone, six pounds was unconfined. Sarah Rudd was five and a half pounds below the upper limit.

There followed another error of judgement. She looked at the photographs of the three physical sizes. The lady modelling to demonstrate a large frame was simply huge; the naked truth was that her flesh was bulging. She must have been a dress size well beyond Sarah. She was size fourteen at a pinch. She hated herself when she selected the more comfortable option of size sixteen.

Sarah blinked at the woman of 'medium' stature. She was well-built. Her upper limit was 147. "Ten stone, five pounds," thought Sarah. She was nine and a half pounds heavier. It was a situation totally acceptable to her husband. It was something she had noted when they were out shopping: his eyes would follow the more well-built women. When a national newspaper focused on 'Rear of the Year' award winner, Nell McAndrew, Nick's interest in current affairs seemed to increase. Sarah had looked at the photographs. Nell ran marathons whilst Sarah had to keep the peace on the streets of Stevenage and survive on canteen food.

Her dietary battles were a daily event. She started every Monday morning with a fresh approach and a revised weight target. The regime generally lasted to Monday evening when, after another demanding day, two children to care for, and a husband who loved talking about his work, she would surrender herself to a bottle of wine and start cutting small pieces of cheese to satiate her hunger. The final thoughts as her head hit the pillow would focus on a revitalised determination and the setting of a fresh weight loss target starting the following morning.

What should she eat? There was no diet, fad, famine, or modern approach she had not followed, all ending in failure. She tried to limit her intake of fats until she reached the police canteen, after hours of trying to deal with the low life of her territory. She would opt for bran flakes with skimmed milk and fresh fruit before returning to the serving hatch and ordering a bacon sandwich. She always had brown bread, although she had little idea why it was better for you. She tried, at home, to keep to white meats, and chicken was their staple food of choice. Fish was becoming more expensive.

There was also the perplexity of her body shape. Sarah's favourite casual outfit was a pair of faded jeans, a thin top and a light beige jacket she had purchased in a charity shop. It was slightly too big for her, and she loved wearing it. The belt holding up her jeans had two notches. She never discussed her waist measurement: that was a secret. The conundrum was that, whatever the weighing scales recorded, this outfit had a mind of its own. She allowed the belt to find its natural home. On some occasions the buckle reached the second notch, the jacket felt loose, and she carried herself with seductive self-confidence. A day or two later, she could hardly find the first notch, the clothing felt tight, and her bottom pressed out of her jeans. It made no sense whatsoever. She even wondered if she had a twisted spine altering her posture.

After several recent battles with the scales, Sarah was beginning to panic. Whatever she did was having little effect on her weight and the disappointment of being over eleven stone bizarrely lead her to binge eat. She decided she must be retaining water, and visited the chemists to buy a diuretic. After being challenged about whether she was suffering from high blood pressure, was she diabetic, and other assorted illnesses, she left the shop in a hurry. She consulted Google, and ended up visiting a health foods outlet. She purchased a pack of pills containing extract of dandelion. She took double the dose and woke up in the middle of night needing to go to the bathroom. These visits lasted hourly until dawn arrived. She stripped off her damp nightwear and leaped onto the scales. The recorded weight was eleven stones, two pounds.

Sarah sat down on the edge of the bath and put her head in her hands.

+

Sarah was in a sour mood. Nick was visiting his parents and had taken Susie with him. She had planned to have a 'kitchen' day, only to remember that she had agreed to take Marcus to Saturday morning football. In view of the unusually mild weather, she chose her favourite outfit. She was convinced that, earlier in the morning, the scales had flickered at ten stone, thirteen and three quarters of a pound before a second reading suggested an additional two pounds. She struggled to pull her jeans up to her waist and then breathed in deeply in an attempt to reach the first notch in her belt. To make matters worse, her favourite jacket seemed to be tight around her chest.

She watched her son take part in a junior kick about before the older boys started the serious game. Marcus was with a group of pals on the touchline shouting for his school team. After ten minutes of the game, Sarah was standing alone when a man approached her and handed over a plastic cup of coffee.

"I've no sugar," he said.

Sarah looked across and accepted the refreshment. "Thanks," she said.

"I'm Greg's father," he continued. "We had Marcus round the other day." He sipped his drink. "What a lovely day," he added. He chuckled. "I'm earning brownie points."

Sarah drank slowly, partly because the drink was hot and partly because her natural caution had kicked in. She slowly turned and summed up the tallish, rather good-looking fellow spectator.

"Brownie points?" she questioned. "Are you a girl guide?"

He laughed and then, to her complete amazement, he lowered his head and kissed her cheek. His after-shave was a powerful aphrodisiac.

"I've seen you several times at the school," he said.

They stopped. A fight had broken out on the football pitch. The referee was blowing his whistle for all he was worth, and several of the watching parents were getting involved. Sarah looked over to see that Marcus and Greg were leading a protest group aimed at a rather unpleasant player on the opposition side. She decided to ignore several of the words she was hearing.

"You have the figure of a goddess," he said.

"If you carry on like this," she said, "I'll have to arrest you for harassment."

"I don't think so, Sergeant Rudd." He threw his cup away. "You're off-duty."

"You know my name?"

"All the men know who you are. We often talk about you."

"You do?"

"You collected Marcus wearing your uniform the other day," he answered.

Sarah chided herself: it was something she tried to avoid because it made her unnecessarily prominent. On that day she had been held up in the front office at the police station and had rushed to the school. She could not understand why Nick could not play a fuller part in the school run responsibilities.

"So why the need for brownie points?" she asked.

"Golf this afternoon, football on the box tonight."

"Your wife must find you compelling," suggested Sarah.

"Second wife. The first ran off with an American."

The referee blew for half time, and Greg's father rushed on to the pitch, where he put his arms around one of the players. They chatted briefly, and then he resumed his position standing next to Sarah.

"Elder son from the first marriage," he said.

Sarah thought carefully and wondered whether it would be sensible to excuse herself from this situation. "That's rather humane," she said.

"What is?"

"Your second wife accepting responsibility for your son from another marriage."

"She'll do anything for me," he said.

"Including watching you throwing yourself at other women," said Sarah.

Marcus arrived, and Sarah paid for him to wander off to the refreshment van and purchase a hot dog. She wanted to ask for one herself.

"My name's Zach," he said.

"Of course it is," replied Sarah.

"Seriously. My parents were evangelists and named me Zachariah. It's a burden I've had to carry with me all my life."

"You don't seem to be doing too badly on it," said Sarah.

"Makes me irresistible, does it, Sergeant Rudd?"

Sarah sighed and felt in her pocket to ensure that she was carrying her warrant card. "I've told you, I'm off duty. It's Sarah, although, perhaps in your case, Mrs. Rudd might be a better option."

She paused and sniffed the air. Marcus and Gary were standing by her, eating their refreshments. She groaned as the hunger pains gripped her stomach.

"We all think so," continued Zach after telling the two boys to go back to the play area and watch the match.

Sarah sensed another male gushing was on its way.

"You're hellishly attractive, and you've the body of an angel."

Weighing eleven stone, two pounds, thought Sarah.

She watched as somebody scored a goal and everybody jumped up in the air. She noticed that Marcus and Gary were hugging each other.

"Marcus told us you are a bit moody," said Zach. "I asked him if he meant temperamental, but he didn't understand the word."

Sarah knew she should end their brief association there and now. She was, however, attracted by Zach's 'in your face' style. He was a handsome man and carried himself with an on-going suggestiveness.

She could never understand why women fell for the men who knew which boundaries to cross. It was a racing certainty that he was going nowhere near the crude suggestions of the sex-starved husbands of whom there were many. He would not mention her underwear and probably make few more personal comments. He had her where he wanted. He had tested her state of mind and was analysing all the answers he had heard.

She had a fairly clear idea of where the conversation would now drift for the remaining twenty minutes of the football match. She decided to stay exactly where she was. Her hands went down to her waist, she breathed in deeply, and she tried to reach the second notch of her belt.

"I don't think they should hang Saddam Hussein," said Zach.

Sarah flared. "I would put him between two horses and send them in different directions," she countered. "I suppose you'll spend huge amounts of legal aid costs reading him his human rights?"

Zach laughed and put his hand on her shoulder. "You, Sergeant Rudd, are just like doctors. Their problem is that they only ever meet sick people." He clapped as the referee awarded a penalty kick. "You deal all day long with criminals." He placed his other hand on her. "You lose sense of the balance a civilised society needs to achieve."

"So what would do if you had to attend a house where the father had raped his eight-year-old daughter?" she asked.

"I live in a street, as you do, where we all exist within an accepted code of conduct, and we all try to raise our kids in a loving sense." He paused. "We are the norm. We must fund the police and social services so that those in the minority, who don't want to play by our rules, can receive help."

Sarah realised that the game was over and Marcus was tugging at her jacket. He pleaded his case that they were going to have an impromptu game on the pitch. Gary was asking the same question of his father. They both ran off, having assumed an affirmative answer.

Zach chuckled. "It's your lucky day," he said. "Let's go and have some refreshments."

Sarah had no intention of refusing his suggestion. They reached the recreational buildings, ordered tea and toast, and found a table in the corner of the pavilion. She spread the butter and jam with a barely concealed gusto.

"I suppose you're one of those lucky people who don't need to worry about their weight?" commented Zach.

"You do seem rather preoccupied by my physical condition," said Sarah.

"'Obsessed' is the word I would choose," said Zach.

"You are wasting your time," said Sarah.

"That's what Saddam Hussein told George W. Bush before he was destroyed by the allied invasion."

Sarah chewed away happily on her sugar-laden breakfast. "Did you support the invasion in 2004?" she asked.

"2003, and no. I was dead against the war, and I was right. It is destroying Iraq and unsettling the Middle East. The whole history of American foreign policy is to go in, especially if oil supplies are involved, win a war, and offer nothing to the peace process that should follow."

"I think John Prescott said something more to the point," suggested Sarah.

"You mean when he wasn't screwing Tracey Temple," laughed Zach. "So what did the Deputy Prime Minister say that impressed you?"

Sarah selected another slice of brown toast, spread a layer of butter, and added two spoonfuls of strawberry jam. She drank her coffee and continued their debate on world politics.

"He was asked about the Middle East conflict and

he said, "They've been fighting each other for a thousand years and they'll carry on fighting each other for another thousand years.'""

Zach nodded in appreciation of the analysis. "It's the old question of 'right' and 'wrong' isn't it," he said. "We were late getting here and I broke the speed limit." He laughed. "I went through the speed cameras at Bowditch Road and, lucky me, they did not flash."

"If you had been involved in an accident, we would have proved your speed," said Sarah. "I suggest you drive within the limits."

She thought carefully to herself. She had seen the schedule of working cameras the previous day at the police station. She thought that Bowditch Road was a target area because the straight road was attracting excessive speeds. She realised that Zach was talking to her.

"Tell me, Sarah. You're a woman."

She chuckled. "You've been brushing up on your boy scout observation books again," she said.

"No. Seriously. Tracey Temple is a pretty, shall we say, well-rounded attractive blonde. Why would she allow a fat lump like Prescott to maul her?"

Sarah munched away and pondered the answer to his question. "I know I said I'm off duty but I'll tell you one thing. We hate being called to domestics. About a year ago, I went to a house on the inner area of Stevenage where the wife had been punched quite badly by her husband. For her own protection, I tried to arrest him, and she then attacked me. They ended up arm in arm."

Zach nodded. He went over to the serving hatch and fetched two further cups of coffee. He took them to the table, and then went outside and checked that the two boys were safe. Zach's elder son had briefly joined them but he had disappeared.

Zach returned to their conversation. Sarah had stood up and released the belt around her waist. Her jacket was feeling tight. She decided to enjoy today and start an unbreakable diet on Monday morning. She smiled as Zach returned.

"Of course," he continued, "in a similar vein, why am I so attracted to you?"

Sarah put her hand on his knee. "I think, Zach, that the answer to that question is rather straightforward. You're just randy. My only protection at the moment is that I'm not in uniform."

"I don't get that," said Zach.

"Men find woman in police outfits a bit of a turn-on."

He nodded. He recalled a recent stag party he had attended where there was a strip-a-gram removing her police clothing.

"I think it's because, secretly, women love attention. That's why Tracey went with Prescott" said Zach.

Sarah stood up. "Time to go home to my loving husband," she said.

"We'll meet again next Saturday," said Zach.

"Will we?" questioned Sarah.

"Today's football match. It's a schools' competition: home and away. The visitors don't have their own pitch so today's game was their 'home' fixture. I've promised Gary I'll bring him next Saturday for their 'away' tie. I'm sure that Marcus will want to be here."

She allowed him to kiss her on the cheek.

"It's a game of two halves," he laughed. "Bit like us, hey, Sarah?"

She watched as he went off to find his two sons. She was thinking about a traffic situation she needed to check.

+

She was naked. Her week had been fraught and the anticipated diet was abandoned at Monday lunchtime after she had attended a horrific accident where an elderly cyclist had been horribly injured. Nick was in a mood because his head teacher had changed his schedule without warning. Susie was teething, and Marcus talked about nothing else but the football match on Saturday. He was now telling her it was time to leave, and she was aware that Nick had taken Susie out in the pram.

She bent her head over the scales and opened her eyes. Never! Never, never, never.

"Ten stones, twelve and a quarter pounds."

She had to stop herself yelling out in unconfined joy. She tried to get rid of the quarter pound by moving her feet on the scales but she was not really bothered. She dashed into the bedroom, put on her underwear and top, and then pulled on her jeans. She actually went past the second notch on the belt. She went over to the mirror. She decided there was a God.

She took her jacket off the hanger and put it on. It was made for her. It hung loosely but with a style that exaggerated her curves. She stood still and looked again at herself in the mirror. She was all woman, and Zach was out there.

They reached the school playing fields to find that the game had already started. Marcus ran off to find Gary, and Sarah ambled up to the side of the pitch. The mild weather was continuing, and she felt a bit special. Within minutes, Zach was at her side. He held her waist and kissed her cheek.

"I've been waiting all week to do that," he said.

Sarah was in a mischievous mood and, afterwards, when she reflected on the success of her trap, she wondered whether she had allowed him a little too much latitude. She also knew that the morning was not going to progress in the way that Zach was anticipating.

"I love your aftershave," she said.

The referee had stopped play and seemed to be talking to two of the players. Sarah looked over and saw that Marcus and Gary were watching the developments on the pitch.

"I really enjoyed our chat last week," she continued. "I'm still trying to work out what Tracey Temple saw in John Prescott and, even worse, you've got me thinking about 'right' and 'wrong'."

"I know. I shouldn't have sped through the cameras and I was lucky," said Zach.

Sarah smiled. "Something that might interest you, Zach." She removed his hand from her shoulder. "A traffic cop was telling me the other day that about a third of drivers cannot remember their vehicle registration number. Fancy that."

"Not guilty, Sergeant Rudd. MP 665 OMR."

"Sorry, Zach. I've got a doctor's appointment on Monday to have my ear syringed. Did you say 'OMR'?"

"Let's talk about you, Sarah. I find your bum

113

absolutely compelling."

Sarah wiped her mouth and rubbed her ear. "Thanks. Did you say 'OMR'?"

"That doesn't matter. I'm going to tell you how I feel about you," said Zach.

"Actually, Zach, it does matter. Can you please stop bullshitting me."

"Pardon?" He hesitated. "Where's sexy Sarah today?"

"It's Sarah Rudd or Sergeant Rudd. You can use either. Now answer my question."

"I don't think I like your attitude, Sergeant Rudd. You police are all the same – you're never off duty."

"Your vehicle registration number is MP 665 OMK. You've doctored your plates and changed OMK to OMR." Sarah continued without interruption. "You've done that because you're a fast driver and you deliberately defeat the traffic cameras in this way." Sarah took a breath. "You're both stupid and dishonest. What example is that to your boys?"

"Prove it," said Zach.

"The traffic cameras are working at Bowditch Road. You were doing sixty-three miles per hour in a forty mph area." She paused. "The ANPR – and, for your benefit, Zach, that stands for the automatic number plate recognition system – couldn't find you because you've altered your plates."

"So we had a social time together, with you sending out all the 'come-on' signals, and then you checked up on me!" he exclaimed.

"It might be my son you kill one day because you think you're above the law," Sarah replied firmly.

"So what are you going to do about it?" asked Zach.

"I'm not going to do anything," said Sarah. "But at five o'clock this afternoon, a police traffic control vehicle will be passing your house and might want to check the number plates of the car in your drive."

Zach glared at her. "I've just remembered I must go and buy my wife a present. She's so in love with me."

Sarah said nothing.

He started to move away but he turned back. "I made a mistake. Your bum's huge. In fact, you're really fat."

Sarah watched him go and realised that Marcus was approaching her.

"I don't understand, Mummy. Gary's father has just shouted at him and pulled him away."

They stayed together and watched the rest of the match. Marcus cheered his side while Sarah allowed her thoughts to reflect on the last two weeks. As another goal was scored, she decided to throw out the weighing scales and just be herself.

Afterwards, as they drove home, Marcus told Sarah that the school side had lost the first match by a single goal but won this morning by two goals, and they were the overall winners.

"You could say it was a game of two halves," suggested Sarah as she stopped the car and kissed her son.

"What does that mean?" asked Marcus.

"What it means, darling, is that what matters in life is who wins."

Marcus thought about what his mother had said. "Do you win, Mummy?"

"Ha! Not always. But today, your school won, and I won."

"How did you win?"

She had pulled up in their drive and Marcus was off to see his father, who was brushing up the leaves.

"Ten stones, twelve and a quarter pounds," she thought to herself and a suggestion made by her Superintendent. It was his proposal that Zach should be effectively warned off.

As she walked towards her husband, she felt happy.

"Perhaps," she said to herself, "a game of two halves followed by extra time after a candlelit dinner for two."

+ + +

IN SPITE OF OVERWHELMING OBSTACLES - JULY 2007

"A hero is an ordinary individual who finds strength to persevere and endure in spite of overwhelming obstacles."
Christopher Reeve (aka Superman)

+

Sergeant Sarah Rudd knew she had to find the time. She saw some of herself in Police Constable Kiddle. She knew there had already been two sexual skirmishes involving the young officer but a colleague, a police constable, who had refused all promotion, reassured her that it "had been sorted."

"I'll drive," instructed Sarah as she and her protégé drove west out of Stevenage towards the one hundred and twenty acres of the Fairlands Valley Park. She knew that Josie was nervous, and she had no intention of putting her at her ease. As they arrived at the sailing centre, they could see that the recreational area was packed with families. Many had brought with them packed lunches to avoid the cost of using one of the franchised food outlets.

They parked the police car, and Sarah locked it behind them. They strolled down to the water's edge.

"Those three children," said Sarah, pointing forty yards to their left.

"Ma'am?"

"How old are they?"

"Erm... I'd say four, perhaps five. The boy is the elder."

PC Josie Kiddle caught on immediately. She went over to the three youngsters and started talking to

117

them. Sarah watched as they all held hands and took the police officer to where a woman was sitting down on the grass, surrounded by carrier bags and speaking on her mobile phone. She had a cigarette in her mouth. Before long they were all sitting in a circle and laughing together. Sarah nodded in approval.

She thought back to December 1998 when, as PC 8377 Sarah Whitson, she found herself in a police car driven by PC Irving Parlin. After he had told her, "You've got a lovely arse, Sarah", an emergency call came in and they attended a school playground incident where they separated two boys, one of whom had a knife. Out of that Sarah acquired a husband and two children. Marcus was now eight and a half, and Susie was heading for her fifth birthday. They had a home, ageing parents, worrying debts, and demanding jobs.

Josie returned.

"All sorted, ma'am," she reported.

Sarah tried to find out how she had handled the situation and smiled to herself when PC Kiddle told her, "I don't do social services, ma'am, I'm a police officer."

They resumed their patrol around the lake, and watched the water sports occupying many of the youngsters present. Josie was a fit-looking woman, and Sarah could see she was savouring the activities. An older couple came up to them and complained about the swearing from a group of boys preparing their canoes. The two OAPs were quite disturbed by the situation. Josie nodded as she watched Sarah defuse their worries.

"How would you have dealt with that incident, PC Kiddle?" asked Sarah.

"Easy," she replied. "I'd have gone into the group of lads and spoken to the taller one of them, the leader. I'd have told him that if there wasn't an improvement in their behaviour, I'd kick him somewhere painful."

Sarah stared at her companion.

"That's Stevie. He's my boyfriend. He's an instructor here."

Sarah looked back at the group now leaving the shoreline. Stevie was clearly the person in charge. He was berating the slowest pair, and she closed her ears to the abuse she was hearing.

"He's off to South Africa for the winter. He wants me to go with him."

Sarah hesitated. There was no way she would decline the offer to spend the winter with Stevie in a sunny climate. She told Josie it sounded like an offer she could not refuse.

"I'll miss the fun," she said. "There are plenty of hunks around, but I've enjoyed the last six months with him. We water ski together."

She wondered about carrying on their conversation in an attempt to avoid the issue which she suspected was coming her way. She decided to remain silent. They carried on walking amongst the families until they reached a quieter area and entered on to a woodland pathway.

Sarah explained she had received a report about an incident three days earlier when PC Josie Kiddle had been part of a team sent in to defuse a city centre fight. At one point a drunken reveller had managed to cut open his eyebrow, and was streaming blood. He had acquired a metal post and threatened the police officer who had become isolated from her companions. The officer in charge mentioned that in the moments before other officers arrived and took down the aggressor, he sensed that PC Kiddle had shown signs of serious hesitation and perhaps intimidation. Sarah asked her junior colleague about the incident and received a clear and honest assessment.

"I was scared, ma'am. It won't happen again," said Josie.

"Scared of what?" asked Sarah.

While Josie pondered the question, Sarah recalled the occasion in February 2000 when Donovan Royle had held her captive and, for several hours, threatened to throw a container full of acid in her face.

"Scared of being hurt? Letting your pals down?" asked Sarah.

"I've always set myself high standards, ma'am," said Josie. "I'm scared of letting myself down." She paused. "After that incident, I went home and was awake all night. I was ashamed of myself."

They carried on until Sarah decided it was time for them to return to their vehicle. As they reached the lake, it became apparent that there was an incident taking place about four hundred yards out into the water. There was shouting, and a woman on the pathway started screaming.

PC Kiddle stripped off her uniform, dived in, and reached the overturned canoe within minutes. A rescue launch arrived shortly afterwards, and all those involved returned to the safety of the land.

As Sarah handed Josie back her clothes, she nodded and scanned her shape.

"Oh, for a body like hers," Sarah thought to herself.

"Impressive rescue, PC Kiddle," she said.

A mother came running up and grabbed Sarah by the arm. "Thank you so much, officer!"

Sarah and Josie made eye contact and they laughed together.

+

The conviviality between the two women was not to last.

Two days later, PC Kiddle was involved in an incident involving a road traffic accident. An elderly man driving a saloon car suffered a blackout, and his vehicle mounted the pavement. It ran into three teenagers smoking soft drugs. As the rescue services concentrated on the four people needing hospital treatment, Josie was part of the team organising the pathway for the paramedics. At a certain point in the proceedings she was holding the head of one of the youngsters who had blood pouring down her face. The report Sarah read suggested that PC Kiddle had abandoned the individual and briefly disappeared.

Sarah discussed the matter with Josie who explained that she had been suffering from a stomach disorder and went behind a wall to be sick. Sarah did not believe her. She was perplexed that PC Kiddle had all the makings of a good police officer and yet there were signs that, at key moments, she lacked the integrity required by front line officers. It was her daughter, Susie, who provided the answer.

Two night later, during the early evening mayhem taking place in the Rudd household kitchen, her husband Nick was trying to open a tin of tomato soup. His hand slipped and two of his fingers were cut open by the serrated edge of the open lid. There was some blood, which Sarah soon had under control, and it was agreed that a simple dressing was all that was needed.

As she turned round, she realised that Susie had turned white and was looking at a small pool of blood on the floor. She started to shake and then to cry. Within half an hour, Sarah and Nick had sorted out the various issues, and the family were having supper together.

Later, as Sarah's head hit the pillow, she thought about the look on Susie's face, and pondered.

The link between the incident and the next action taken by Sarah was so tenuous as to be fanciful. Throughout her career she challenged convention and was prepared to take chances. She spoke to the police surgeon, who agreed to meet with PC Kiddle. A few days later the doctor and Sarah met at his surgery.

"How do you do it, Sergeant Rudd?" asked Dr Matthews.

Sarah smiled. "You have an answer?" she asked.

"Definitely. Your police constable is suffering from haemophobia."

He went on to explain that 'blood phobia', as it is more usually called, is not a phobia but is a biological condition. "Your daughter was upset by the sight of blood but is unlikely to be affected in the longer term," he continued. "In Josie's case, she has always been a fitness enthusiast. In her late childhood she suffered from a series of nose bleeds."

He stopped and took out a paper bag containing peppermint sweets. Sarah put her hand in the packet and took two. She popped both into her mouth.

"This is quite common and nothing to cause

concern," he continued. "However, in her case, her mother panicked and took her off school. To make matters worse, this happened on several occasions, and Josie missed out on the swimming championships." He paused. "Here it gets more complicated. In the funny way in which memory and the brain works, my guess is that whenever Josie sees blood, a chemical reaction takes place in her brain." He laughed. "We have a name for it. We call it 'vicarious childhood trauma.'"

"Heavens," commented Sarah.

"Of course, she does not know this and, in her own mind, she is defining it as personal weakness."

"But you have explained this to her," said Sarah.

"No. I need to discuss it with you."

"Why?" asked Sarah.

"You see a healthy young woman, attractive, athletic, the world at her feet."

Sarah remembered her diving into the water at the lake. "She's impressive, yes."

"She's a mass of contradictions. But worst of all, she's lacking self-esteem. What she wants more than anything is to believe in her future as a police officer."

"Which means what?" asked Sarah.

"Can't you reassure her on her prospects?" asked Dr Matthews.

"No, I can't," replied Sarah.

"You're not willing to help her?" he asked.

Sarah stood up rather abruptly. "Can you reassure me that if she is faced with the need to protect a member of the public she will stand firm?"

Dr Matthews glowered. "Can you sit down, please, Sergeant Rudd."

Sarah did as requested, but asked for a glass of

123

water. The doctor provided her drink, and seemed keen to talk further.

"We can counsel her," he said.

Dr Matthews explained that a process, wherein the individual learns to raise their blood pressure, had helped certain sufferers of haemophobia. This is achieved by squeezing the larger sections of muscle groupings in the body. The increased tension acts as an antidote to the phobia.

Sarah stood up again. "Thank you, doctor. I realise you mean well."

Dr Matthew spluttered. "You mean you aren't going to let me try?" he exclaimed.

Sarah turned and faced him. "The solution to this situation, doctor, can only come from Josie herself. She'll have to dig deep and, to be candid with you, I can't give her much more time."

+

Josie Kiddle was in a sour mood. Not only was Stevie going to Australia, but he had dumped her by text message. She stared at her phone and drank her glass of wine. She blamed herself. Stevie had wanted a carefree, physical relationship which included going to South Africa. She had wanted to talk.

The wine bar was busy with Friday night revellers, but she was alone. She listened as Kate Nash sang about 'Foundations':

"My fingertips are holding on to the cracks in our foundations,

And I know that I should let go, but I can't..."

Stevie had let go, and she was isolated in her thoughts. Here was a conundrum for her to puzzle over as she poured herself another glass of wine. Why do police officers bother to get married when the divorce rate is so high? The canteen was a Mecca for affairs. A sergeant who had taken an avuncular shine to her had told her it was the pressure factor. Police officers are thrown together in stressful situations which seem to act as aphrodisiacs.

She drank deeply. What had Kate Nash suggested? *"Everything's fine, except you've got that look in your eyes, When I'm telling a story..."*

Josie decided that a more likely explanation was that all they really wanted to do was talk about 'the job'. She suspected that, at times, Stevie was only pretending to listen to her, and really his thoughts were elsewhere.

It had crossed Josie's mind that she might be bisexual. She was seeing Faroda at the water sports club more regularly, and they had started to go for coffee. They talked at length about her job and Faroda's adherence to Muslim teachings. Then there was PC Nathalie Payne. They had joined at the same time and often found themselves together. She was two stone overweight and was forever dieting. She could laugh at herself and Josie loved that. Once, during an evening patrol, they had found themselves holding hands.

Then there was Sergeant Sarah Rudd. She was the role model for Josie. She had the lot. Josie wondered whether, after she had stripped off and dived into the lake, Sarah had been eyeing her near naked body.

"It's the only free seat in the place; can I have it, please?"

Josie looked up. She liked his face. He was modern: shaved head, two-day stubble, and clean. He seemed genuine. She could not see any other vacant seats.

She smiled back, and he sat down. He put his glass of lager on the table and looked away. Amy Winehouse was singing about a problem:

"They tried to make me go to rehab but I said 'no, no, no."

Josie looked at her phone, but her text messages were empty. She had decided against replying to Stevie. Each response she composed became more morose. She looked across at her table companion.

"I'm going to get myself a drink. Save my place?" she asked.

He took out a twenty-pound note and tried to hand it to her. "I'll buy it", he said.

"No thanks," replied Josie as she departed towards the heaving crowd surrounding the bar. She returned about ten minutes later. He was still sitting there, with a second full pint of lager.

"My sister bought it for me," he said as he realised her surprise.

"She sounds a doll," said Josie.

"She's the cause of all my problems," he replied.

Josie laughed. "If you drink too much, that's your problem. Bit cheap blaming your sister, isn't it?"

"Mescaline," he said.

Josie searched through her memory bank. She knew the name and immediately linked it to a talk they had been given by the drugs officer. For some reason the word 'Vicodin' came into her head.

He had started to explain things to her. His name was Jack. He organised overseas sporting tours, mainly cricket, but also golf, rugby union, and athletics. He did not touch any football matches whatsoever. He explained that there were a growing number of retired people, mainly men but an increasing number of women, who were healthy and wealthy and wanted to travel the world. The growth of cricket's 'Barmy Army' had been a poster board goldmine, and he now employed nine staff.

He paused and drank deeply. Josie decided to sip her wine and listen to Jack. His body language suggested pent-up emotion, and she knew there was some pain on its way.

"About six months ago one of my overseas organisers went bust, completely out of the blue. I thought I had checked everything. I was out of pocket by twenty thousand pounds, and then I read the small print in my insurance cover."

He banged his fist on the table, and Josie wiped a few drops of wine off her hand.

"The bastards not only didn't pay out but they increased my fucking premiums."

"You're wearing some smart clothes and you seem to have a supply of twenty-pound notes so I've worked out that you solved your problem," suggested Josie.

He ran his hand over his perspiring head. "I'm going to get a drink. What's yours?" he said.

"You've had enough," said Josie. "Sit down."

He sat down.

"Men," thought Josie. *"Putty in my hands."*

"So you found twenty thousand pounds?" she said.

Jack stared at her. "What do you do?" he asked.

"I'm in insurance," she replied.

"Oh". He wiped his mouth with the back of his hand. "Why are you on your own?" he asked.

"I'm particular," said Josie. "Where did you get the

127

money?"

"From my sister, in a way of speaking."

She stood up. "I'm going to allow you a half of lager which I will buy," she said. "But first I want your car keys."

Jack laughed. "Have you driven a Ferrari before?" he asked.

"No. My Honda is fine for me. But neither are you driving your car tonight. Are we agreed on that?"

He put his hand in his pocket and took out the ignition keys. He held them up in the air, "One condition. You buy me a pint."

Josie took them and put them in her pocket. She stood up and re-joined the mayhem as closing time approached. She returned some time later with his drink, a large glass of wine, and several bruises.

Jack sipped his pint but then drank deeply. "I don't know your name, Miss Insurance Clerk," he said.

Amy Winehouse had been replaced but the sound was drowned out as voices became louder.

"What's the connection between your sister, mescaline, and twenty thousand pounds?" asked Josie.

"Are you a fucking detective?" responded Jack.

Josie stayed silent and stared at his face. She knew he was going to tell her his story. A drunken youth toppled over and into her side. Jack flared up. She simply spoke quietly to him and he went on his way.

"Zeeta is into soft drugs. Nothing serious. Not hard stuff. But she found a supplier who sold her a drug called mescaline. It's a psychedelic and more usually called Vicodin. It comes from a cactus plant grown in Peru." He drank the last of his lager. "I was desperate and it all quickly escalated out of control. I

128

met her contact, and started to deal. I made quick money. As long as I paid them their bucks, all was fine." He paused. "I knew it was wrong. I was desperate. I said I would pay off the money I had lost and stop."

"Which you have done."

"I had the chance to double the size of my business. I reasoned that it was justified because I'd employ another six people. It's taking time."

"And you can't pay the dealer," finished Josie.

"They're getting heavy. What the hell is your name?"

"So what are you going to do?" she asked.

"I'm going to the police in the morning."

Josie breathed a sigh of relief. "Is that the drink talking?" she asked.

Jack put his hands to his face and took several moments before replying. "It's Jack talking," he said. "I have to do it, for Zeeta's sake."

"No," said Josie. "She'll be fine. Do it for yourself. Wipe the slate clean and rebuild your business."

Jack looked at her. "You're not an insurance clerk, mate. Who the hell are you?"

The question remained unanswered because, although the bar was emptying, two men were approaching where Josie and Jack were sitting. Josie instinctively knew that they meant trouble. As he reached their table, the first pulled out a knife. He reached across, grabbed Jack by his collar and yanked Jack towards him. Somehow, his hand was jarred backwards, and the knife sliced open the corner of his eyebrow. Blood poured out, covering his face and shirt.

"You owe us fucking four grand, Jacky boy," he

spluttered.

He let go as he held his hand to his face. The other, dark-skinned, man remained menacing but still. Jack toppled backwards and Josie leapt up so she found herself between the two assailants and a cowering companion. As she watched the blood pour down his face, she tried hard to tense her muscles to stop herself shaking. She felt warm urine running down the inside of her thighs.

"Put your weapon down," she ordered.

The Londoner stared in surprise.

"And what are you going to do about it, Miss Red Riding Hood?" he sneered.

"I'm Police Constable Josie Kiddle of the Hertfordshire police."

Jack looked at her in complete amazement.

"I'm going to give you one more chance. Put the knife down."

Two police officers had now arrived in response to an emergency services call from the bar proprietor. They radioed back to Control that they thought PC Kiddle was involved in the incident. Within three minutes, Sergeant Sarah Rudd had arrived at the scene.

The drugs dealer from Hackney sneered at Josie. "Lover boy owes us fucking money. Now fuck off before your face changes shape."

The two officers had taken their truncheons out. It was two months before selected forces were due to begin testing the use of the Taser gun.

"She's a woman, a kid. She's out of her depth. We'll go in," yelled PC Sands.

Sarah Rudd gave him a look comprising poisoned daggers. "You'll stay where you are," she ordered.

"But..."

"Stay where you are, constable," repeated Sergeant Rudd.

Jack was now on his feet and trying to persuade Josie to leave things to him.

The knife-wielding thug resumed his verbal onslaught. "Fuck off, beautiful. We're going to slice up your friend."

Josie dug deep and stood up to her full height. "To do that you'll have to go through me," she said.

He stared at her and hesitated. She saw her chance. She lashed out and kicked him viciously in his groin.

"Now!" shouted Sarah.

The police were there in a flash, and the two men were taken down. As they were being handcuffed, Josie's foot was just a few inches from the hard man's face.

"Not a good idea, PC Kiddle," said a voice.

She turned and saw Sergeant Rudd smiling at her.

"I'll stick with the thought, ma'am." She held up her hand, and looked for her companion who was just a few feet away. "This is Jack. He wants to talk to the police." She looked at him. "Is that right, Jack?"

He nodded his head and tried to speak, but he was already being led away.

+

"What are you doing, PC Sands?"

The police officer laughed. "I'm sitting down. You asked to see me. Obviously you're pleased we got a result last night."

Sergeant Sarah Rudd stood erect. "Stand up, now," she commanded.

131

He hesitated, fatally. "But you..."

"You call me Boss or Sergeant Rudd. Stand up." She circled round him. "What did you mean, PC Sands, when you said, "She's a woman, a kid." What did you mean?"

"I didn't mean anything... er... Sergeant Rudd. The guy had a knife. She was in danger. I thought we should go in."

Sarah Rudd shuddered with anger. "What you meant, you monstrous lout, was that poor little PC Kiddle was a woman and needed beef like you to protect her."

"She did well, Boss. She was brave."

"You really want me to get angry, don't you?" said Sarah. "She was an off-duty police officer who showed more presence of mind and courage than you ever will. If I ever again hear you make any sexist remark, you'll wish you had never heard of me. Now get out!"

+

They were walking together by the side of the lake. Sarah knew that Stevie was in the past. They found themselves strolling in the autumnal winds.

"How have you been, Josie?" asked Sarah.

"I'm in good shape, ma'am," she replied.

"This chap, Jack. Am I right that you had only just met him?"

"That evening. He sat down in the only spare seat in the bar and we started talking. He clearly was upset and told me about his business problems and that he was peddling in soft drugs."

"And what did you do?" asked Sarah.

"Well, in truth, he talked about giving himself up. This was before the thugs arrived."

"Did he know that you were a police officer?" asked Sarah.

"He thought I was an insurance clerk."

Sarah smiled. "It's not my decision but if you felt able to testify to what he said, it could help."

"A shorter sentence, ma'am?" asked Josie.

"Jack's simply lost his way. He's not a criminal in the way we mean. Dealing is serious, even soft drugs. We have to charge him but the Crown Prosecutor thinks a probationary sentence is possible. Waste of time and money sending him to prison."

"Is that what will happen?" asked Josie.

"It's possible." Sarah hesitated. "Are you sure that you should involve yourself, Josie? Why not give him some time and space to sort himself out."

"I'd like to see him again," she said. She paused. "There was something... it's crazy, I suppose, but in the time we were together I felt closer to him than I ever did with Stevie."

Sarah remembered when she had stripped off and dived into the lake to rescue the children from the overturned canoe. *"And I bet he'd like to see you again,"* she thought to herself.

"Don't get hurt, Josie. Now he knows you're a police officer."

Josie stopped and turned towards her superior. "Did you say I'm a police officer, ma'am?"

"There's some paperwork to do, but the result is not in doubt."

Josie strode ahead, trying to hide her gasp of relief. She turned back. "Something strange has happened. I received a bunch of flowers."

"I wish my husband would buy me flowers," thought Sarah.

"From Jack?" she asked.

"From PC Sands. There was a card. It said, 'Well done from us all'."

Sarah nodded in approval. "Is it 'goodbye Jack?'" she asked.

"Oh no!" Josie said, "I've had several text messages." She laughed, "And anyway, I've got something he wants."

"I'm sure you have," thought Sarah.

"What do you have that he wants, PC Kiddle?" she asked.

Josie put her hand in her pocket and pulled out a set of car keys. She waved them in the air.

"Mustn't keep a man from his Ferrari," she chuckled.

END OF PART ONE

PART TWO

AN ACCIDENT IN TIMING - DECEMBER 2008

The torrid relationship between Sergeant Sarah Rudd and Dr Martin Redding

They never knew what led to the accident that resulted in the motorway traffic grinding to a halt. The deluge of snow, which subsequently engulfed the stranded motorists on the A1 (M) north of London, ensured that the emergency services were overwhelmed. They were hindered by drivers who blocked the hard shoulder with their vehicles. It was a December weekday in the late afternoon; it was getting dark and becoming colder. Two individuals, each with their personal challenges, were trapped together. From within their cocooned isolation, they were to face a choice which could have a shattering effect on their lives.

+

"Damn."

Sarah Rudd had already turned the heater control of her Vauxhall Astra to full, and the windows of her car were still icing up. She knew she should have taken the vehicle in for servicing, but they could not afford it. She and Nick had around two hundred pounds left on one of their credit cards, and she had reserved that for the household bills. When both their salaries arrived in their bank account there would immediately be an outflow of payments, leaving them little money remaining for Christmas.

The tension between the two of them had exploded the previous weekend. They had received another letter from the Northern Rock Building

Society. They did not really understand the financial crisis and why the government had been forced to rescue their lender. What they did know was that their mortgage repayments had been doubled because their 'interest subsidy' period had ended. The additional six hundred pounds a month repayments simply crippled their free cash position.

Sarah had attacked Nick for betraying his children. She remembered every single word he had told her. She reminded him of his repetition of the phrase 'the end of boom and bust', as trumpeted by the Chancellor of the Exchequer, Gordon Brown. She held back from expressing her disappointment at his lack of promotion as a schoolmaster. She wondered if he loved his work, and she was in no doubt that he was a diligent and successful teacher – perhaps rather too much since he apparently lacked the drive for self-development. Occasionally, in her lowest moments, she decided he was simply too nice a person.

She did not hold back from expressing her opinion when she finally spoke to a call operator at the building society. Her anger was fuelled by their telephone answering system, which required her to make several choices, then push button six, and wait and wait whilst she listened to the music of an obscure American folk singer. The interruption every two minutes that "your call is important to us" added to her volcanic mood. When, "Jack, I'm here to help you," came on the line, they started off in a fairly responsible way. That was before they began a descent into a deep subterranean pothole of pent-up resentment.

Sarah's well-prepared line of attack had been to

question why their repayments had doubled when the Northern Rock Building Society was receiving subsidised funds from the government. Jack was ready for that one. He told Sarah that they were not actually using any government funding, ignoring the cost to the British taxpayer of the original rescue. He was baffled by Sarah's suggestion that, "you should bloody well be using it, then our repayments could go back to the level you conned us with."

The downhill momentum gathered pace as Jack firstly suggested that they sold their house, and then reminded Sarah that if they missed a repayment their credit rating might be affected.

"You're fucking blackmailing us," she cried.

"There will be a letter in the post to you, Mrs Rudd," concluded Jack.

"Fuck you," Sarah said to herself as she slammed down the phone. Nick was standing there, preparing to go out for a run. Sarah looked at him with utter disdain.

They had virtually no money and few unused credit card limits to pay for their children's Christmas.

+

She shuddered: it was too cold to be wearing just a skirt and tights. She had her coat on but it was not sufficient to provide her with the warmth she wanted. She rubbed her thighs and remonstrated to herself for the reason her legs were exposed. She had never lost the discipline of dressing respectably for her mother. She also knew that her beloved father would not say "no".

She grabbed her iPad and read the latest traffic

news. She could expect to be marooned in the middle lane of the north bound A1 (M), north-west of Stevenage, for at least another hour. She was on her way to see her parents, following her mother's fall down the stairs. The scans had shown severe bruising but confirmed that nothing was broken, so the hospital had discharged her. Nick was not expecting her home until around ten o'clock. Sarah had put an overnight case in her boot, just in case she needed to stay longer. She assumed that Marcus and Susie would be in bed and asleep by eight o'clock; at least Nick was a reliable father.

To make matters worse she'd left her mobile on her desk; it had been a hectic day at the police station. Sarah was not at her best and she was frustrated by her on-going domestic tensions.

There was a tapping on her window. She looked out and saw a snow-covered person gesticulating. She lowered the window.

"Hello. Just checking you're alright," said a muffled voice.

Sarah laughed. "I'd invite you in but my heater's on the blink and I don't have a phone."

A helicopter flying above distracted them: the pilot's passenger was providing the police with operational information.

"The traffic is not going to move for some time, so come and join me," replied the stranger. "My car is warm."

Sarah was street-wise on the issue of personal safety and decided that not much could happen in a car in the middle of a traffic jam on a crowded motorway.

She closed the window, got out of the car,

wrapping her coat around her. It was two short strides to the open door of the black BMW. She settled in and gave out a loud sigh of relief. She observed that the inside of the vehicle was immaculately tidy: no sweet papers, no opened sandwich containers, no plastic bottles; no human debris of any sort.

"I've not locked my car," she announced. She watched as the passenger side window descended. She pointed the key at the green Astra and thought that she heard a clunk-click. The headlights briefly illuminated the van in front. It was one of the new knights of the road: 'Javelin Home Deliveries: reliability is our guarantee' said the phosphorescent sign on the back doors.

"Not this evening," thought Sarah.

"Would you like some water?" asked her rescuer. "It's sparkling."

She took the plastic bottle and gulped three mouthfuls. She was beginning to relax, and assessed her temporary companion. She decided that he was in his early fifties, handsome, clean-shaven, dark hair with a dash of grey, and wearing dark trousers and a black jacket.

"Hercule Poirot has nothing on me," thought Sarah. What did the Belgium sleuth say? "It is the brain, the little grey cells on which one must rely."

"Better introduce myself: Martin," her companion said. "Martin Redding." He laughed. "As we might be stranded for some time, you've got to guess what I do."

"We'll be here for an hour or more," said Sarah holding up her iPad. "That's the latest estimate." She smiled. "I'm Sarah Rudd."

"How's the temperature?" he asked. He then noticed that she was wearing a skirt.

"I'm feeling more comfortable, thanks," said Sarah. "You're a vampire," she suggested.

"Not bad," he replied, "but I hope it's not reflective of my work." He shook his jacket and straightened his shirt. "I'm a doctor. My practice is in Highgate."

"*Strange clothes for a doctor to be wearing,*" thought Sarah.

"You're going the wrong way," laughed Sarah, "North London is the opposite direction."

Their attention was diverted as they became aware that a group of people was gathering behind the car. Martin reached for his coat on the back seat, got out, and joined the others. He returned a few minutes later.

"The British at their best," he said. "The HGV drivers are checking all the cars and vans to ensure everyone is safe. They've spoken to the police who can't get through at the moment."

"Can I help?" asked Sarah.

"Everybody is fine, but I guess we'll have another meeting. There seems to be a consensus that, as you said, we have an hour's wait ahead of us. There are possibly dead and injured people in the accident ahead so it will take time to sort it out."

As Martin settled back into the warmth of his car, Sarah made a proposal.

"I guess we'll have to talk about ourselves," she said.

+

The snow began to fall more heavily, and the whole area remained static. The traffic on the southbound carriageways was also stationery. On the far side, flashing blue lights showed that an emergency vehicle was making some progress.

"Music?" Martin said, reaching for the CD player.

"Elton John," suggested Sarah.

"Can't abide him," laughed Martin. "I can offer Rachmaninov, Lloyd Webber, or *Simply Red*."

"If you play Rachmaninov's second piano concerto, we can act out our own brief encounter," said Sarah.

"And I'm the doctor getting something out of your eye," chuckled Martin.

Sarah allowed her thoughts to wander. In the film 'Brief Encounter', Laura Jesson knows that Fred, her husband, is honest and reliable, but she's bored with her middle-class life. A chance meeting at Milford railway station with Dr Alec Harvey leads to a passionate affair.

"Anyway, that film had a sad ending. She went back to her husband," he said.

"No, it didn't," said Sarah. "Celia Johnson had no choice but to go back home to her children."

Martin shook his head. "She was frustrated with her husband. She should have gone off with Trevor Howard. They were madly in love."

"They hardly knew each other," cried Sarah. "It was all about lust. They wanted to be in bed together."

"They'd fallen in love," argued Martin.

She withheld further comment as the opening bars of the Rachmaninov concerto played out. Had she been able to read the notes on the CD cover, she would have shared the writer's opinion that the concerto offered, 'the spontaneity of a memorable melodic invention with its exquisite craftsmanship.'

Sarah settled back into the leather seat, beginning to feel more relaxed, and listened to the music. The warm air was flowing up her thighs, and she was feeling friendly. She decided that what was happening was unlikely but was real. She realised that a few tears were forming in her eyes as she recalled the final scene of one of her favourite films.

She was Laura peering out into the smoke-filled railway station and hoping beyond hope that Alec had not left to go to Johannesburg but would re-appear on the platform and she would fall into his arms. But he did not materialise, and so she went home to husband Fred and her children.

"*You're wrong,*" Sarah mused to herself. "*She was bored and wanted physical affection. She would never have left her family, parents and friends.*"

+

Sandra Redding was focused. She had told her husband to read up on it before they discussed her proposal any further. It was, in fact, not a suggestion: it was an ultimatum. She was cross that Martin had still not mastered the different meanings. **Polygamy** *is, in essence, having a number of married spouses at the same time regardless of their gender.* **Polygyny** *is one man with multiple wives where society, and the law, permits it.* **Polyamory** *means having many committed relationships. Sandra did not help her cause by telling her husband that he had to accept* **polyamory** *and that it came from the Greek* **poly** *meaning 'many' and the Latin* **amor** *meaning 'love'.*

Her logic was overwhelming. They had married late and,

after the birth of their son, she had decided that she did not want to experience childbirth ever again. For a number of reasons, but mainly Sandra's unspoken opposition, the possibility of adopting was discussed and discarded, and she threw herself into her two dogs. Her father's inheritance ensured they had no financial concerns. Martin was well-paid. They had three holidays a year, and shared a love of water sports. Their bedroom had once been a place of contentment.

A year ago, Martin became aware of some subtle changes. Sandra started to dress differently, and her charitable work seemed to take her increasingly away from home. He was busy and ignored it. When, one evening, she asked him to sit down in their kitchen, he had no idea what was to follow. Her name was Ingrid, and Sandra was in love with her. She would be moving into their house in two weeks' time. She realised that Martin needed to agree to this and she did not think it would help if he bombarded her with questions. She dismissed any possible damaging effect on their son who, as Sandra succinctly observed, was shagging his way through medical school. She had asked for an answer within two weeks. He said she had to tell him what the consequences would be if he said "no." She had replied that she was certain that would not be his answer.

+

Martin was a long way away from reaching a decision. He did not understand how he was supposed to offer possible solutions to his patients' complex conundrums within a ten minutes' surgery consultation, when he was a dithering heap after trying to resolve Sandra's demands. It was farcical that he had been pushed into this position. Did it matter whether it was polygamy or polyamory? They should have adopted children. Two King Charles

Spaniels were not an adequate substitute.

He became aware that he was becoming sexually aroused. He also knew why. Her thighs were stunning. Her skin had a hypnotic quality with a slightly oily surface. Her skirt was riding up and an occasional blast of heat only served to inflate the material.

Sarah quickly pushed it down again. She had removed her coat and put it on the back seat. She was wearing a white blouse, and he could not resist glancing at her pink bra. He must concentrate on her face. This resulted in further challenges because Sarah was seductively attractive. Much of this was natural; in modern terminology, her DNA. She thought she was carrying seven pounds too many, but it did not seem to matter. She was not to know that that Martin had put *Rachmaninov's* No 2 piano concerto on repeat. She was aware that her skirt was once more inching up her thighs. She decided to do nothing about it.

+

After forty minutes of their enforced captivity on the A1 (M) motorway north of London, their body language was telling all.

Rachmaninov had given way to *Simply Red* and Mick Hucknall was crooning '*Oh! What a Girl!*' On two occasions, Martin had re-joined his fellow travellers in the snow, and there were reports that a diabetic woman, around a hundred yards back, needed help. The police had now reached her and an ambulance was nearing the scene. Up ahead, good progress was being made by the rescue services and it was thought that the traffic would begin to move in about thirty minutes' time. The experienced HGV veterans said that that would mean their section would be underway in about forty-five minutes.

They had each turned towards the other. Martin had produced a second bottle of water and a tin of fruit drops. There were nine left, which worked out to four each. They decided that the remaining one (blackcurrant) would be awarded to the person who could say the most interesting word that the other could not define. He produced a ten pence piece, tossed it, Sarah called 'tails' and lost.

She allowed her thoughts to wander back to home. When had she and Nick sat down together and been silly? Their conversations were about financial pressures, the childcare roster, their parents, his lack of promotion, and her success as a police officer albeit that he would always change their direction of travel at that point in time. They never discussed their barren relationship.

"Tautological," suggested Martin.

Sarah laughed. "You didn't say this was to be an intellectual game," she cried, slightly excitedly because she knew what it meant. "Saying the same thing using different words," she answered.

"Wrong," cried Martin.

"Bloody right!" said Sarah. "Where's the referee?"

"You, my failed contestant," said Martin "have defined the noun. Tautological is the adverb."

Sarah groaned. "Men," she said. "Right, I was correct and it's my turn." She pretended to be deep in thought. "Ah ha. Sarah is about to win a blackcurrant fruit drop. Ready?"

"Can't wait," answered Martin which was exactly how he was feeling except he was not thinking about blackcurrant fruit drops.

"Physiognomy," she said.

"You're disqualified," he yelled. "That must be a medical term. How can I be expected to know that?" He put his hand on her thigh, "I'm only any good with coughs and sneezes."

Sarah left his hand where it was. "Hand it over," she said.

"Hang on. Give me a chance. 'Physio' means natural study so it must be a reference to... er... 'gnomy'. What the hell does that mean?"

Sarah threw her arms up as much as the restricted space of the car would allow. "I am the champion," she cried.

This had the consequence of the buttons of her blouse coming under pressure from the landscape underneath and her skirt riding high over the crossbar, so revealing pink knickers. Martin groaned with pain.

"Physiognomy," he said, in an attempt to regain normality. "I don't know."

"Give," said Sarah, holding out her hand. She popped the sweet into her mouth, seducing him even further. "It's the study of people's faces to judge their character."

It was one of the few things that she remembered from her recent training course on the techniques of the police interview.

"Now, why would you know that?" he asked.

Their banter continued as Mick Hucknall suggested that "Something Got Me Started".

+

It had started to snow again, and they were still stranded as they waited for the traffic to start moving. Following their light-hearted quiz, they lapsed into a period of quiet reflection. Martin had found a CD of ballet music, and the soporific sounds seemed to subdue their earlier frolics. He thought that he was making polite conversation when he asked Sarah why she was wearing light clothing on a winter's day.

"I'm going to see my mother and I feel I have to wear what she thinks is appropriate." She smiled. "Do you usually ask a strange lady about her clothing?"

"Seems a reasonable question to me," chuckled the doctor.

"What are you suggesting?"

"Nothing at all. I'm just puzzled that a rather impressive, sensible woman is taking personal risks with her health." He paused. "The flu at this time of year can be a problem."

"It doesn't rank with my real problem," said Sarah.

Martin's professional training took over. He remained quiet. The patient will always tell all if let alone.

"We've no fucking money," she said. "I'm pretty sure my mother is fine, although I do what to check her over."

Martin's impatience took over from his professional stance. "So the respectable skirt, the tights, and the pink underwear is for your father?"

"Yes. He's always been a bit of a lad. I know he played around but he gave us a wonderful home and upbringing, and my mother accepted the deal." She paused. "Anyway, you know the saying: "A man can have affairs. What he can't do is not provide for his family." Sarah wiped her eyes. "I'm going to ask him for a thousand pounds."

"Phew," said Martin. "What will he say?"

"Nothing," replied Sarah. "He'll give me a cheque."

"How will your husband react?" he asked.

He hesitated as a police car travelling on the hard shoulder stopped opposite them. This was followed by a tapping on his window. He lowered the glass, and spoke to the officer who asked about the unoccupied car in the middle lane.

"That's mine, officer," said Sarah, "My heater is on the blink so I've been sheltering in here."

He shone a torch in her direction. "Your registration number, please," he asked.

"Perhaps you should look at this," she said as she handed him her warrant card.

Satisfied by her reply, they had a brief conversation, and he moved on after saying there were further delays and that they could expect to leave in about forty-five minutes time.

Martin wound his window back up. "You're a police officer."

"At your service. Sergeant Sarah Rudd of the Hertfordshire police."

"Heavens," he said.

+

When Sarah Rudd and Martin Redding were to later individually reflect on those life-changing two hours on the motorway they, individually and collectively, concluded that the experience gave them an opportunity to express themselves. Both professionally and as individuals, they knew that the subjects of sex and sexuality are two of the most sensitive subjects for human beings to discuss.

There is a basic reason for this. A majority of people immediately adopt a position based on their upbringing and beliefs. What most men and women want is a shared, loving relationship with a life-time partner where their sex lives take place behind closed doors and are never mentioned. The modern world allows greater promotion of gender change, homosexuality, feminism, and the rest of the media-driven diversions. Websites encouraging planned adultery and sexual liaisons flourish. Other websites allow new relationships to begin and many prosper. The internet allows unrestricted access to the most depraved pornography imaginable.

But, in their individual situations, Sarah and Martin reflected the basic modern conundrum. Each wanted a close, bonded togetherness with a member of the opposite sex and, behind closed doors, to experience rampant lustful sex without any guilt.

Martin started to tell Sarah about the decision he was being asked to make by his transgender wife. She sank back into her seat and, although her skirt once more rode up her legs, she was aware that the atmosphere was changing. They were bonding; brought together by unrelated events.

"Are you aware of Jung's theory of synchronicity?" asked Martin.

Sarah was sucking the last of her fruit drops: strawberry. She nearly swallowed it whole. "Not a day passes without me worrying about it," she said.

"He was an Austrian philosopher and his great belief was about 'meaningful coincidences'. What he basically said was that, in life, two unrelated events can come together to produce a result."

"I bet he was a wow at dinner parties," she said.

"It gained credibility in the film '*The Eagle Has Landed*'," he continued.

"With Michael Caine," exclaimed Sarah.

"From the book by Jack Higgins. Hitler orders the capturing of Winston Churchill and at the same time Agent Starling in East Anglia reports to the German High Command that Churchill is visiting the area. The German officer describes it in terms of Jung, a 'meaningful coincidence'."

"This is scary," teased Sarah. "Do you think he's with us today?" She paused, and stared at Martin. "Do you imagine we're having a Jung moment?"

"What do you think, Sarah? You're not hiding your lust, and I'm being asked to accept that my wife will now sleep with a woman."

"Do you think that, Martin? Is that your worry? Sandra is off to bedrooms new?"

"I've asked the question. She blanks me on it."

Sarah paused and stared at his appearance. "Martin," she asked. "Why are you wearing a black jacket?"

He sighed. "Because I'm on my way to a singles evening. One of these websites. A patient told me about it."

"And what will happen?" she asked.

"My expectation is that I'll meet someone, have sex with them, and go home."

Sarah sighed. She then suggested that he was retaliating. When he questioned her line of accusation she explained that he was trying to get his own back on Sandra.

"You don't want to sleep with some strange

woman," she said.

"I'm not sure that I can face life without her," said Martin. "She's the only woman I've ever loved." He wiped an eye. "I feel I've let her down."

"How have you done that?"

"She's had to find fulfilment with another person."

"Is the problem that it's a woman?" asked Sarah.

"No. I can live with that. Society is dealing with homosexuality much better these days. I think it's unnatural and, in the scale of things, it only involves a few people. Most are heterosexual and get on with their lives."

She paused and finished sucking her fruit drop. "I'm not sex starved, Martin," she said.

He remained silent and instead focussed back on her thighs. She was becoming even more tantalising as her face relaxed.

"You are, or else you'd not be here. You'd have gone back to your car when I put my hand on your leg." He paused. "What I think your greater need really is, is affection."

Sarah looked out of her window and at her car. It seems so cold and isolated. In a few minutes time, she'd be back in the driving seat, crawling her way to see her parents.

"We do have options," suggested Martin.

"We do?" replied Sarah.

"We'll be moving soon. One mile ahead is a junction that leads to a hotel I occasionally use."

"Use for what?" she asked.

"They usually have rooms available," he said. "We have two hours free. You are not due home until ten o'clock, and Sandra doesn't care where I am."

"I'll be able to seduce you by taking off my tights,"

said Sarah.

"For starters," laughed Martin.

Sarah was thoughtful, and remained quiet. Outside, the snow had stopped and the lorry drivers were starting up their engines.

"I'm not sure," she said.

"I understand that," he said. "I have a suggestion to make."

"Another one," laughed Sarah "What's Jung up to this time?"

"You get into your car and think about what I'm proposing. As we drive off, if I see you indicating to leave the motorway, I'll know you have decided to accept my offer."

"And will you chat me up, Martin? Please convince me that romance is still alive."

"You'll think Daniel Craig is in the bedroom," he said.

"Three in a bed, is it? This is getting interesting."

+

The debris had been cleared off the A1 (M) Motorway. A wife was on her way to identify the mangled body of her dead husband in the mortuary, and three people were receiving hospital treatment: one would be detained overnight.

Sarah had started her engine, and much to her surprise, the heating system was beginning to clear her windows. She looked across to her right, but Martin was staring ahead. She was a mixture of emotions. "Jung was right," she thought to herself. "This has been a meaningful coincidence. I want sex and Martin wants to retaliate against Sandra." She laughed. "Two hours in a hotel bed will sort out everything," she decided.

He was watching her drive away, and he moved over to the middle lane to be behind her. There were about one thousand yards to go before the exit signs would appear.

At 900 yards, he began to have doubts. He wondered whether he should fight for possession of Sandra. They were, in their own way, close. He did not want to have to start again. There were the odd dalliances in hotel rooms but then again, he knew for certain that his wife had strayed in their early days together.

At 700 yards, Sarah was going weak at the knees. Was it too early to start indicating? She did not want to lose him. She would email her father about her late arrival, email Nick and tell him she'd be staying overnight with her parents. Her hand hovered over the indicator lever.

At 500 yards, Martin was beginning to perspire with lust. She had a sensational body with the few extra pounds that men love, she was fun and naughty, and she wanted sex. He praised his pal Jung for his perspicacity. He groaned in anticipation.

At 300 yards, Sarah was not so sure. She was thinking about her husband. He was a lovely man and the father of their two children. She was sure they'd find a way through their financial mess, and she'd put her uniform on for their bedroom frolics.

At 200 yards, Martin decided to say "yes". Sandra could have Ingrid but he'd so love her, she'd come back to him. In the interim he'd sort out the short-term physical needs. Hell, those thighs.

At 100 yards, Sarah was becoming angry. It was

Nick's fault. He was neglecting her, and it was time to do something about it.

At 50 yards, she reached for the indicator control. And then she had second thoughts.

Martin peered ahead. The snow was falling again. He spotted her car. Was that an orange light flashing on the passenger's side of her car? He simply could not be sure...

What he could never have known was that, at a much later date, Dr Martin Redding would try to kill Sarah Rudd.

END OF PART TWO

After 2009, Sarah Rudd's eventful career is told in a series of City thrillers:

'Megan's Game'
'The Deal'
'Cholesterol'
'A Flash of Lightning'
'The Lady Who Turned'

In the second part of 'The Lady Who Turned', Dr Martin Redding re-appears. Sarah Rudd leaves both the police force and her husband, and becomes a private detective working in London.

What follows is one of her early adventures...

PART THREE

THE CONTRACT KILLER - OCTOBER 2015

He was going to die, and everyone accepted that nothing could save him. Everyone, that was, except former police officer Sarah Rudd who did not agree with this assessment. But she was proposing a course of action against all the odds...

+

"You were fucking around and you screwed my father," shouted the voice coming from the phone ex-Detective Chief Inspector Sarah Rudd was holding away from her head. Her son, Marcus, continued his verbal assault. "We don't miss you. Susie hates coming to your drab Knightsbridge flat." He paused. "Dad's happy now you've gone." She heard the sound of the phone being slammed down.

Sarah had phoned her son because he had not acknowledged his fifteenth birthday card and present. As he had made no reference to the substantial cheque she had sent, she realised the writing was on the wall. She had been too busy to buy a present. The telephone rang again. Her former husband, Nick, spoke quickly. "Sarah. Hold on. Please don't put the phone down."

"Did I deserve that, Nick?" she asked.

"No. Susie lives for the time she spends in London. Marcus does not know about my Australian girlfriend. We came apart. That was all, Sarah."

"And there's nothing else?" she asked.

"Marcus had a problem at school and the local police got involved. It's all sorted. I think he's only got you to take it out on."

"Are you in good shape, Nick?" she asked. "Is there anybody else in your life?"

"That's off-side Sarah. You chose to leave for London. End of relationship. End of story." He put the phone down. Then it rang again. "Sarah. I didn't mean that. I'm always here for you." This time the phone call ended, for good.

She collapsed onto her sofa, turned up the music, and resumed drinking her vodka and tonic. She had anticipated the events of the last few minutes. She had always known that there would be short periods of pain and depression.

Max and his passion was no antidote at this stage. He'd arrive later. She was where she wanted to be: a valued member of the Delamount Security team. She realised that her robe had come open, and she was spilling the alcohol down between her breasts and towards her femininity. It tickled her.

"What you need, former Detective Chief Inspector Rudd," she said out loud, "is a juicy case which only you can solve." And then she started to weep.

+

Hello suckers. Bet you don't understand the term 'short selling'? It's one of those opaque terms the City of London financial centre uses. It disguises the probability that you, the hapless punter, are about to be conned out of your hard-earned money by smooth-talking operatives. You'll be so hypnotised by the words and the promises, you'll get sucked in and screwed. What you need to know is that the advisers, the directors, and the original investors will have stashed away their profits long before you, the sucker, get a sniff.

The latest wheeze the boys are exploiting is, and always has been, personal pensions. The Government ministers in the Treasury have created a bonanza for the swindlers. By the time it is exposed, they'll be in the House of Lords, rich beyond belief, and with the chairmanship of a quango to ensure they don't have to pay for their holidays. It is called the democratic system. Just to make you feel even more jealous (or angry – your choice) it is said that a peerage is like giving somebody an annuity of one million pounds. Failed/sacked government ministers get peerages.

Sorry, I should have introduced myself. My name is James. Well, actually, it isn't. It's a disguise because I kill people. I'm a contract killer. I suppose I should call myself Carlos, or 'The Jackal', or perhaps Murphy, even 'Mad Dog'. I thought about Boris, but one madman of that name in London is enough. James works for me, so that's that sorted. Please don't call me Jimmy. He's taken over four hundred wickets for England and I haven't.

I kill my victims in one of two ways: either by blowing up their car with them inside it (usually making identification near impossible) or by shooting them, close up, using a silencer. Once in the back from behind. It takes about four to five seconds to cause death, by which time I've disappeared. I kill people (usually male although I did eradicate a transvestite recently) because I'm paid to do so: about £100,000. The money is sent to an offshore account in Port Vila, which is the capital of Vanuatu. You might have heard of the place as the New Hebrides. It's in the South Pacific and there are eighty islands or thereabouts. The northeast coast of Australia is nearby. Nobody pays any income tax in Vanuatu.

As I am talking to you, I'm opening a 'special delivery' envelope. There is a sheet of paper, some brief details, and a photograph. I'll be quite pleased to assassinate this bugger: Bartholomew Hamish Walkden. Probably a wealthy patriarch, public school, the City and the rest. £100,000 already dispatched to my bank in Port Vila. I have seven days to blow up his car with him inside it.

Please convince me that you are not tiring. Every crime writer these days invents a killer. The difference is that I'm real. I was a City trader in Moorgate. We were fiddling everything possible. Give me an index and I'd manipulate it. There were twenty-three of us making, on average, several million pounds each year for ourselves. We didn't do recession. We just made more dosh.

The boss lived in South Africa. Out of the blue, one of my colleagues turned. His wife had become an evangelist and took to leaping up and down praising God. She intoxicated him with her beliefs, silly girl. He started talking to himself at his desk, and then suggesting what we were doing was immoral, which it was.

He then announced he was going to take a few days off but, on his return, he expected he would have no choice but to make a statement to the Financial Regulator.

I use my money to ensure the continued companionship of Lily, my stunning but expensive lover and partner: her speciality is orgasmic meditation. I also collect first editions of an artist of whom you have never heard. I have six investment properties, three cars – you get the picture. And this born-again Christian was not going to queer my pitch. I flew to Johannesburg and met with the boss. We agreed that there was only one answer. He paid me £100,000 and I returned to London; within a week I had killed the bastard. It was surprising how easy it was to buy a weapon, though having friends in the Army helped, as did my ability to hand over lots of money.

Out of the blue, my boss asked me to fly out to see him; he helped his cause by sending me two first-class plane tickets. Lily celebrated by putting on her Mediterranean bikini and lighting the incense sticks. My reply was delayed by an hour as we improved our OM technique: I'm the stroker and Lily is the strokee.

When we arrived, and after being wined and dined (did she turn him on!), I sat in his study and he made me an offer. He sometimes needed to eradicate opponents and used London contacts. He suggested I took over the role; I could expect up to six instructions a year.

On each occasion, I would receive a plain envelope and brief but sufficient information; I would make no attempt to identify the source. After the contract was completed, I would destroy all the information I had received. There would be a simple code indicating whether the assassination was to be achieved by a shooting or a car bomb.

After I had undertaken five contracts to his satisfaction, he would pay me a bonus of one million pounds. If I ever betrayed a confidence, I would be dead within forty-eight hours.

The third time involved, for me, the first occasion that I used an explosion to destroy a car and the occupant. Once more, the simplicity was frightening (especially for law-abiding citizens). There was a puzzling moment when the boss said that the instructions I would receive would not necessarily come from him. That was three years ago, and I have now completed nineteen contracts. They always come in a plain white envelope, and I have no knowledge of who has sent them to me. On two occasions there have been difficulties but I have found I am rather adept at dealing with the unexpected.

My wealth is increasing, and Lily and I are enjoying the high life. I'm nervous about taking holidays, so we limit ourselves to long weekends in Monte Carlo. My bank circulates the fees received in Vanuatu back to a hedge fund in London, which is doing rather nicely.

Time for me to eliminate Bartholomew Hamish Walkden.

+

Norman Delamount came forcibly into the meeting room on the first floor of the offices of Delamount Security. He stared at Sarah Rudd and Max Hemmings.

"Sarah, please meet Tub." He beamed his welcome. "Sarah was Detective Chief Inspector Rudd, a brilliant police officer."

Former DCI Sarah Rudd looked askance. The visitor to Delamount Security was slim, tanned, and handsome. At six foot three inches and one hundred and ninety pounds, he was not overweight. Former Detective Chief Inspector Max Hemmings took an instant dislike to him. He was not bothered that he had not been introduced.

"Tub needs urgent assistance, and has asked that his situation remains confidential from me. I suppose I buggered him too often at Harrow." Norman roared with laughter. "Tub," he continued, "these two are my best team. Trust them and be completely honest." With that, he left the room.

Tub sat down without being asked.

Sarah poured some coffee and pushed the cup towards him. "Tub?" she asked.

"My father is a Companion of the Bath because of his position in the Civil Service; he was a Permanent Secretary in the Home Office. I went to Harrow where they put bath and tub together to reach my nickname. I'm never called anything else." He shrugged. "Better than Bartholomew."

"What does your family call you?" asked Sarah.

"My father has disowned me, and my mother is dead."

Max looked up after completing some written notes. "Norman does not use the term 'urgent assistance' without careful thought, Mr Walkden," he said.

"Please call me Tub. I'll get to the point as to why I am here. I'm going to die in the next five days."

Sarah gripped the edge of the table and put her hand on Max's sleeve. "Are you ill?" she asked.

Tub laughed and stared at the two former police officers. "That's the point!" he exclaimed. "The problem I have can be cured."

Sarah moved her chair and faced their visitor. She offered her maternal smile. "I think, Tub, it would be best if you tell us your story. We won't interrupt you," she promised, giving Max a warning look.

Bartholomew Hamish Walkden turned his chair and faced Sarah. "I'm not a pleasant person, DCI Rudd."

Sarah let the error go.

"I work in international finance and make piles of money." He coughed. "My methods are sometimes, shall we say, ruthless, and these days it's much more difficult to move cash around." He hesitated again, and looked furtively at Max. "For that reason I know some rather unpleasant people. Their loyalty can be fragile and I occasionally use the services of a contact in Haringey. I pay him a sum of money, give him brief details, and a few days later somebody disappears." He paused and drank some coffee. Sarah sensed that Max was ready to interject but he found a hand pressing down on his knee.

"Recently," continued Bartholomew, "I needed some hospital tests. Last Thursday, the consultant said I had an incurable growth in my lower stomach. They could manage the pain, but there was nothing else to be done. I pressed him, and he thought I might have two to three months left. He said the cancer was spreading quickly." Tub paused and wiped his forehead. "I have been with my wife for twenty-three years, and we have two children. I decided that I could not put them through what I knew they would face. I enquired about that place in Switzerland, the Dignitas Clinic, but the formalities are prohibitive in my situation. There are also some personal tax situations which could affect Avril's financial position. If I commit suicide, it will leave the family with all sorts of complex issues."

He stood up and started pacing around the room. Sarah was warming to this man. Max sensed trouble.

Bartholomew ran his hand through his fair hair. "It may sound stupid," he said, "but I'm scared of dying. The actual last few moments – you only begin to understand this when you are facing the reality. You might find that difficult to comprehend."

Sarah recalled the time when Donovan threatened to throw acid in her face, and her recent escape from death at the hands of the deranged Dr. Martin Redding.

"I came up with a simple solution," Tub continued. "I put a contract on myself. I would be blown up in my car, and I would not know a thing. The coroner, in all probability, will rule it murder by a person or persons unknown. The police won't try very hard because they will know it was a contract killing and their chances of finding the guilty party are rather slim." He paused. "The money has already been paid," he said. He drank some water that Sarah had poured for him.

"Well, that's that," said Max. "I suggest you go and get yourself blown up, and let me get with some important work."

Bartholomew smiled. "I sensed immediately that you did not like me, Mr. Hemmings." He laughed. "I suppose you and I have been on opposite sides for too long."

"You're a fraudster, a killer, and much more. I have spent my professional career trying to lock up people like you," snapped Max.

"You're also a client," said Sarah, glaring at Max. "Norman says we are to try to help you." She smiled. "I sense you have more to tell us, Tub."

Bartholomew turned back to her. "The day after I put out the contract the hospital contacted me urgently. I rushed to see the consultant. Somehow, the test results had been mixed up. I had a growth but it was non-cancerous, and he could operate. He said I should make a full recovery." Bartholomew grimaced. "The doctor could not understand why I wasn't in raptures over his news."

"And you can't stop the contract?" Max asked.

"If I make any attempt to interfere with the process, I'll be eliminated. There is nothing I can do."

"Leave your car in the garage," suggested Max.

"The rules are that if there are any difficulties, the killer can use his discretion. He'll find me and shoot me. It's the worst possible result."

"Your contact in Harringay. Surely you can talk to him. Offer him money?" suggested Sarah.

"It doesn't work like that, Sarah," said Max. "Tub can't go near him. He'd be wiped out instantly."

"So what do you think we can do?" Bartholomew let Sarah's question hang in the air. "Norman owes me a favour. A big one. If anybody can sort this out, it's him."

"And we are Norman's proxy. But we can't talk to him?" said Max.

"No, you can't, and no more questions, please. Either you can help me or else I'll go away."

"To be blown up," said Max.

"It's the best solution for my family," he said.

+

Hello again, lemons. While I must spend some time preparing to eliminate Bartholomew Hamish Walkden, I will not insult your intelligence by informing you how to make a bomb. It's so simple, some of you might well know the procedure already. The difference between you and me is that I live well and you don't because I'm rich and you aren't. My guess is that you have fee-loaded mortgages, credit card balances coming out of your ears (take lots of free-transfer offers, did you, suckers?) and unpaid bills.

Some of you are divorced because you thought the grass was greener. That's your ex-wife in the Mercedes spending your allowance. The other thing that you do, and I don't, is pay tax. You are middle-class muppets. You are the most heavily-taxed people in the world courtesy of our one-nation government.

You are the favourites of Her Majesty's Revenue and Customs because they have you every which way they want. Your earnings are taxed at source (and National Insurance, to welcome in the immigrants), if you remove a pencil from your desk you'll face a 'benefit-in-kind' payment, if you sell an asset you'll pay 28% capital gains tax. The best bit of all is that every year you have to do all the work and tell HMRC everything.

Have you ever met anyone who has been the victim of one of their inspections? Talk about 'guilty until proven innocent'—which you won't be because they'll find something. Have you seen their rulebooks? There are four encyclopaedias of them.

What about VAT at 20%? The rich (the Conservative Party and the BBC) don't care because they're rich. The poor don't care because they have huge benefit payments and steal what they want. Drug dealers don't care because they've got so much cash.

I know things are bad for you and so I think I'll make them worse. Lily and I have a modern relationship. You won't understand that because you are monogamists. Put that another way, you are trapped by your conventions and taboos. You have boring or non-existent sex lives, and you are desperate to screw a woman you know but the consequences are inhibiting.

Let me help you escape. Read 'Sex 3.0: A Sexual Revolution Manual', by my mate JJ Roberts. I met JJ in Durban when he was researching 'unfenced relationships'. I must be mad; I'm giving you all this advice and not charging you. Still, I can afford it, and you can't, because you are middle-class, debt-ridden puppets of the upper class called the Conservative Party.

Back to killing Bartholomew Hamish Walkden. It really is a piece of cake. He parks his car, registration number BAT 41M, in the street outside his Mayfair home. The CCTV coverage is good so I'll need to be careful. The trick is that at 6.30am in the morning, nobody cares. The bomb is prepared, and I'll move in two days' time.

+

Norman Delamount manifested his anger with controlled sarcasm. His reddening forehead and lowering eyebrows added to the sense of conflict erupting in the Board Room of Delamount Security.

"So, you clowns, two of Scotland Yard's former leading detectives cannot solve a minor issue."

"I never was at Scotland –"

Sarah was interrupted by his fist hitting the top of the table and the bottles of water flying in several directions.

"Tell me, Norman," said Max, "what's this hold that Bartholomew has over you? It would help to understand that."

The owner of the security business seemed temporarily flustered. "It's irrelevant, Max," he spluttered. "It's nothing to do with you. Something from the past." He hesitated. "Tub has telephoned me. He was abrupt, and said that you two were negative."

Max laughed. "We are not permitted to tell you his problem, and you refuse to confess what his hold is over you." Max paused. "And we're the problem, Norman?"

Norman stood up and spoke to Sarah and Max in a quiet voice. "The two of you have until the end of tomorrow to prove to me that I should continue employing you."

As he pushed his way out of the room, Sarah turned to Max.

"I can't afford to lose this job," she whispered.

"Let's walk in the park," he suggested.

+

Hello again. It's me, James. Sorry to interrupt your paperwork as you try to work out how to pay your bills. You'll have already settled your tax because HMRC are at work while you sleep. You will have heard that second-rate House of Lords peer talk about the wealth divide (because he is chairman of a government committee investigating it that will achieve nothing but earn him more dosh; the going rate is £250,000 per annum).

Well, lemons, shall I tell you who is the biggest enemy to a fair society? Tax accountants! They have a sole purpose in life: to ensure their clients don't pay any tax (or as little as possible). All that claptrap about evasion is a crime and avoidance is legitimate. Tell that to those prunes who financed highly dubious films for the sole purpose of not paying tax.

The fiscal (that's an impressive word for tax) legislation is so complex that highly paid accountants work through the small print in the legislation (the annual Finance Bill) and devise clever ways to confuse everybody: HMRC, the judges and so on.

Answer this question: why do footballers pay so little tax? Because they are rich beyond belief and can afford to employ the top tax accountants who make sure they pay as little as possible. How can Wayne Rooney be a brand?

In case you are worried I'm not paying attention to my work, Bartholomew Hamish Walkden will die at 6.45am on Thursday morning. I'm not prepared to let you in to my trade secrets, but Thursday morning is the best time to kill somebody. Did I tell you that the money is already in my Vanuatu bank account? Well, some is but about £70,000 is being used by a pal in the City. He specialises in putting out false rumours about public companies after he has sold the shares. He then buys them back at the lower price and pockets the difference, tax-free of course. It's called 'short selling'.

You sell something you don't own, spread false rumours (a crime but nobody ever gets prosecuted), and then buy it back at a lower price. Clever clogs in the City, aren't they? We'll make about £40,000. You won't clear that in a year because of all the tax deductions you face, and yet, a few months ago, you voted for a Conservative MP. You think I have a chip on the shoulder about this matter, don't you?

Write to your MP and ask him what pension he will receive

when he retires. His (or her) reply will avoid answering the question because it is HUGE! You won't do this because you are too knackered at the end of a day's work and you know your own pension is likely to be around £2,000 per month and it's taxed. By the way, the financial adviser who looks after your pension makes a fortune. I know. I did that until I found an easier way to accumulate more wealth (untaxed).

+

Sarah Rudd was alone in her Knightsbridge flat. Her marriage to Nick was over and she was left with the weekend visits of her daughter, Susie. She was having sex with Max but she was a long way from moving in with him.

They had spent the afternoon in Hyde Park, talking through the conundrum facing them.

Max had forced the issue with Norman Delamount, who finally admitted he had had a homosexual partner not known to his family. The relationship had foundered, and his lover tried to blackmail him with some photographs taken when Norman was knocked out by champagne. Bartholomew had sorted things out.

"So, Norman is a killer," said Sarah.

"The murderer was the person who completed the killing," said Max.

He shuddered slightly as the autumn sun disappeared into the western sky. He tried to put his arm around his colleague. Sarah shook him off and stood up.

"We're giving in too easily on this, Max," she snapped.

"Norman is hooked because he had his former

lover killed. Bartholomew is a swindler, a fraudster, and a man who has people eliminated. I don't care a fuck that he's going to die."

"But we are professionals. We have a brief from our boss. We have no choice."

Max stood up. "Sarah, we do. Norman has always said we are free to decline any mission he offers us." He stood to his full six foot two inches. "I decline," he said. He gave Sarah his special smile. "Shall we go for a meal?"

"You go home, Max."

"A Sarah sulk, is it? Have it your way."

"Norman is the boss. We have a job to do."

Max grimaced and wiped his forehead. "You may do, Sarah, but I reject it," he said as he walked off towards Park Lane. But then he turned back. "Seriously, Sarah. Are you comfortable that our boss paid to have a man killed?"

She looked at him expressionlessly. "I like the job, and I need the money," she said.

+

Completing my checklist. Bartholomew Hamish Walkden will be dead in the morning. The Financial Compliance Officer at a firm I once slaved away for used to have a risk-assessment strategy. He had to complete a checklist before he said "yes" to anything. Idiot. As I knew the questions he would ask, it was rather obvious I would have the correct answers prepared.

My risk-assessment is as follows:

+ have I been paid? (Confirmed)
+ have I been paid a lot of money? (Confirmed)
+ will I pay any tax? (No)
+ is there any chance of not killing the victim? (5% at the

most)

+ will I escape? (Yes; usual disguise and I'll be detonating by remote radio)

+ is there any moral issue? (You're joking)

+ do I love my life? (Yes, and Lily, and my first editions)

Time to sign off then. I'm glad that I'm rich and I'm sorry that you aren't. That's life and you did, of your own free will, vote Conservative. I read that another batch of cronies are becoming peers of the realm: about thirty-five of them.

Lots more millionaires talking patronising waffle in the House of Lords. Over eight hundred of them, with an average age of seventy. I'm told they form a vital part of our democratic system. They didn't stop Tony Blair invading Iraq, did they?

+

For the first time since their separation, Sarah was missing Nick. How many times had she benefited from his words of wisdom as she struggled to solve a crime?

Her hand wavered, and then she dialled the 'home' number. His voice melted her, and they compared notes and discussed their children: he confirmed that Marcus's problem, whatever it was, was solved. Sarah told him about the situation involving Norman and Bartholomew. She realised afterwards that he did not mention Max. Did that mean he had somebody else already?

Sarah was not to know whether he chose his words deliberately, but when he said, "It sounds to me like somebody has to die," he unleashed the genius that had established the outstanding career of DCI Sarah Rudd.

+

That's it then. Almost all over. He'll be dead shortly. What an explosion it'll be. I have checked my mixture carefully. Bye muppets. Enjoy paying your taxes. One final political thought. The UK has the eighth highest national debt in the EU. Call it the Chancellor's time bomb, to be ignited when interest rates go up. The members of the Lords don't care. Nothing threatens their bloated pensions.

+

Sarah and Max were watching 'Breaking News' on the SKY early morning programme. There been a serious explosion in the Mayfair area; the emergency services were in attendance. Norman Delamount came storming into their room. "I heard about it in the car. Tub's gone. You're fired. Get out, both of you," he shouted.

Sarah stood up and walked over to the lounge entrance. "There's somebody here to meet you, Norman."

"Get out, Sarah. I thought you might have found a way to save him."

She opened the door, and ushered in Bartholomew Hamish Walkden.

"Tub!" yelled Norman.

"The very man, Norman, thanks to your gifted colleague."

"I've always said Sarah is the special one," beamed Norman.

"She'll be joining Chelsea, next," thought Max. "So, if you weren't in the car, who was?" he asked.

Sarah spoke quietly. "He was called Martin, and I'm not telling you his surname. He had about two weeks to live, and no money to provide for his family." She handed Norman a piece of paper. "I'd like £100,000 sent to that bank account, please, Norman."

Bartholomew took the slip out of her hand. "I'll do that," he said.

"So what happens to you, Bartholomew?" asked Max.

"I died in the car, Max. I'm flying to Belgium for stomach treatment, and once I've recovered, plastic surgery. I'll be back in six months' time. My wife and family are wealthy, and the taxman will get nothing. You didn't like me before, so I suppose the facial changes will make no difference."

Max turned and walked out of the room.

+

Christ, I've never known pain like this. I'm lying in this disused garden. The fucking bomb. It's never happened before. Didn't explode. I edged nearer and nearer, and then up she went. The fragments sliced me open as I went backwards. One hit my mouth, and now I can't make a sound. I crawled down a passageway and now I'm lying in some shrubs. There are bits of me coming out below: a long piece looks suspicious. It's getting dark when it shouldn't be. I'm cold. God, I'm scared. I can hear voices...

+

"So we have your husband to thank for this," snapped Max.

Sarah stood up from the park bench, and walked around for a few moments.

"Don't do the 'arrogant Max' bit, please," she said. "You fucked up. We had a job to complete for

Norman, which is why he pays us. You became all judgemental. It was not your place to decide whether Bartholomew lived or died. What did we learn as police officers? There were crimes and there were processes. We followed the rules."

"Always?"

"I was lucky, Max. In my chat with Nick, he said, probably without realising what he meant, that somebody was going to die. I simply worked out that we could complete our task if the person who died was not Bartholomew. I went to a home for the terminally ill in Sloane Square. The man I found was the seventeenth person I spoke to. All he could talk about was that he was leaving nothing for his family. His business had failed, and then he caught something nasty on a trip to Africa. The only issue was that he was so ill I wondered if he would last.

"He had to discharge himself so I suppose they are now looking for him. I managed to get a coat and hat that Bartholomew wears, and he just about made it to the car. I had obtained a duplicate key from Bartholomew. I watched the killer place the bomb. He did it at 3.00am. I had to be sure there was no chance of an identification of the victim, so Tub had organised with a contact to have explosive placed inside the vehicle earlier in the day. The resulting explosion simply eradicated the man beyond any identification."

Max remained thoughtful. He wanted to tell Sarah that she had, yet again, shown herself to be a brilliant detective. He sensed he had disappointed her. "Dinner tonight?" he suggested. He looked again at her body language and slowly walked away.

+

Good news muppets. They've reached me. The way this Government is wrecking the National Health Service, I'm amazed. Your taxes will be going up to pay for it. I don't pay tax, you lemons. My last message to the world. The Government are covering up the true indebtedness of the NHS. Barts Health has a £150 million deficit... shit... I can't feel my feet. To be honest I can't feel anything... my eyes are closing...

+

Sarah was watching a television news programme. A reporter, live from Mayfair, was explaining that the explosion earlier that morning had destroyed a car believed to belong to City trader Bartholomew Walkden. His family had been informed, and were receiving counselling.

The scene switched to further along the street and an area cordoned off by police tape. The reporter struggled to remove her wind-swept hair from in front of her face. She revealed that a body had been found alongside a terraced property; the police were appealing for witnesses who might have been in the area in the early hours of the morning.

Sarah switched off the television, and replaced it with the music of Andrew Lloyd Webber. She found herself drinking a glass of vodka and tonic more quickly as Colm Wilkinson pleaded that they 'Bring Him Home'. Sarah thought about her son, Marcus.

Was she a 'Miserable'? She had no regrets. London and the Knightsbridge area was intoxicating for her. She had strong feelings for Max, and the sex was good. She had simply outgrown Nick. She needed time. She was focused on absorbing herself in her responsibilities at Delamount Security.

Sarah was confident that she was good at what she did. What she could not know was that, within months, she would be faced with a hostage situation that would dwarf everything else she had experienced in her career. She would have to choose between saving the life of her lover, Max, or rescuing four starving Syrian refugee children from drowning in the English Channel.

She poured herself another glass of vodka and added a dash of tonic. The mixture of music and alcohol was making her randy, and she decided to plan the next occasion with Max. She was becoming aroused, and started to feel happier.

And, anyway, Susie would be arriving tomorrow.

The End

Look out for more City adventures featuring Sarah Rudd and her special brand of policing.

If you would like to be notified when the next book is released, be sure to sign up for my free newsletter at:

tonydruryemailsign-up.gr8.com

THANK YOU!

To my Reader:

Many thanks for buying and reading the *Journey to the Crown - The Career of DCI Sarah Rudd from 2003 – 2008* short stories. I hope you enjoyed reading these insights into Sarah Rudd's career.

If you did enjoy, please post a review on your favourite social media site and let your friends know about *Journey to the Crown - The Career of DCI Sarah Rudd from 2003 – 2008*.

I hope that this has whetted your appetite to read the novels in the Sarah Rudd City thriller series. You can find details of these in the next few pages.

And don't forget to sign up for my newsletter for details of my latest books and a FREE short story!

tonydruryemailsign-up.gr8.com

Happy Reading!
All the best
Tony

ALSO BY TONY DRURY

Sarah Rudd City Thriller series

Sarah Rudd stories

Sarah Rudd Short Stories

Stories written for **HEART UK – The Cholesterol Charity. (All publisher's profits are paid to the charity)**

Hannah's Choice

Joanna's Choice

Mark's Choice

The Dinner Party

The Novella Nostalgia Series

Lunch with Harry

ABOUT TONY DRURY

Tony is the author of five DCI Sarah Rudd City thrillers. In each, he draws upon his career as a London financier to expose the underworld of dark practices and shadowy characters. None, however, are able to withstand the bravery and incisive detection methods of one of the police force's bravest officers. Her juggling of career demands, husband, children and her own demons, make riveting reading.

He has now written two more novels which trace the early career of probationary police constable Sarah

Whitson. In 'On Scene and Dealing' she meets her future husband Nick. In 'Journey to the Crown' she has a devastating affair with Dr Martin Redding. The final chapter jumps ahead to sample her future life as a private detective.

Tony has created an innovative series as a novella writer. Reflecting iconic cinema classics, his first is 'Lunch with Harry', which is inspired by 'Breakfast at Tiffany's'. Others to follow include 'Twelve Troubled Jurors' (echoing '12 Angry Men') and 'Forever on Thursdays' (capturing the drama of 'Brief Encounter').

He writes short-stories wherein the net proceeds go to HEART UK – The Cholesterol Charity. He is an ambassador for the charity.

Aged seventy, Tony is a follower of the wisdom of Albert Einstein: "When a man stops learning, he starts dying." He lives in Bedford with his wife Judy. They value every trip down the M1 to Watford to be with Grandson Henry.

Connect with Tony online:
(e) tony@cityfiction.co.uk
(w) tonydrury.com
Twitter: mrtonydrury
Facebook: facebook.com/tony.drury.author
Goodreads: goodreads.com/TonyDrury

Lightning Source UK Ltd.
Milton Keynes UK
UKOW05f2221080317
296165UK00009B/233/P